He is the principal of his own boutique law firm, Bennett Bankruptcy Law, in Toronto, and bankruptcy counsel to other law firms. He is well-known in Ontario and nationally. His practice is focused on all facets of creditor and debtor law, asset protection, enforcement of judgments, receivership, bankruptcy, and restructuring. He advises debtors, creditors, trustees, and monitors.

For many years, he was the Head of Section and Lecturer for the Ontario Bar Admission Course on Creditors' and Debtors' Rights and Remedies, Lecturer in other Bar Admission Courses including Family Law and Real Estate, the past Chair of the both the Bankruptcy and Insolvency Section of the Canadian Bar Association, National and Ontario, a veteran council member of the Ontario Bar Association and member of several committees, a former member of the Bankruptcy and Insolvency Advisory Committee to Industry Canada, a frequent lecturer and author of several books and articles on creditor and debtor topics. He has received honours from the Law Society and from the Bar Associations.

To Janice Faith, the love of my life.

Franklyn Harris Bennett

SUBMISSION

AUSTIN MACAULEY PUBLISHERS™

LONDON ★ CAMBRIDGE ★ NEW YORK ★ SHARJAH

Ordering Information
Quantity sales: Special discounts are available on quantity purchases by corporations, associations, and others. For details, contact the publisher at the address below.

Publisher's Cataloging-in-Publication data
Bennett, Franklyn Harris
Submission

ISBN 9798886939774 (Paperback)
ISBN 9798886939781 (Hardback)
ISBN 9798886939798 (ePub e-book)

Library of Congress Control Number: 2023913753

www.austinmacauley.com/us

First Published 2024
Austin Macauley Publishers LLC
40 Wall Street, 33rd Floor, Suite 3302
New York, NY 10005
USA

mail-usa@austinmacauley.com
+1 (646) 5125767

Table of Contents

Chapter One
Parliamentary Committee Room

Ottawa: House of Commons Committee Meeting Room—Royal Commission on Family Matters in Canada. The room is a large cavernous area with tables set up in a U formation. Committee Members around the tables are Members of Parliament, their assistants, Law professors, members of the Family Law Bars of each province and territory, and representatives of the Canadian Bar Association, provincial and national colleagues.

The gallery is filled to capacity. Mostly women from the Ottawa area, but some from Toronto and Montreal.

The Chairperson bangs his gavel on the desk.

"Silence, please."

A few seconds delayed.

"This is a Joint Committee of the House of Commons to study the ongoing violence in domestic relations including protection of spouses and children. Apart from myself, being a Liberal MP, there are two other members of Liberal caucus, two members of the Conservative caucus, and one member representing the New Democratic Party.

"As you will hear, part of our problem is the conflicting and overlapping jurisdiction of the Federal Government regarding divorce and the provincial and territorial governments over family support and protection. While somewhat protected, family break-ups have slipped through the cracks causing untold grief to our citizens and their families."

The Chairman then introduces Louis Gonsalus, a retired long-time Member of Parliament. Mr. Gonsalus stands up and approaches the lectern. He takes a drink of water and then begins narrating a story.

"Mr. Chairman, Members of the Committee, distinguished guests, and witnesses, I confess that I have become a cynic of our Federal and Provincial

Governments over the years. I suggest to you that we have let our guard down in not protecting family relationships and family values. We are truly behind the times. And we are paying for it now, with divorce rates significantly up, one out of two marriages, family and domestic violence with attendant criminal charges, marriage breakups, and inadequate support tools for children and spouses.

"Let me tell you a story that has become all too common in Canada. Let me tell you the toll it has taken on the families and especially the children. It is not an unusual story, but a usual one. One that is happening every day across Canada. And that's why we are here today. To review the situation publicly; to make suggestions and to see them implemented, in my lifetime."

Picture this.

Highway 400, Heading North to Muskoka

Two cars heading north on Highway 400 from Toronto to Muskoka a day before the long holiday weekend in July. One car, Thomas (Tom) and Elisabeth (Beth) Richardson chatting about the commercial still photography business and their fading personal relationship. Background music: Vivaldi, summer. The other car, Richard and Wendy Richardson, Brother and Sister, and Melissa Rothbart, friend of Wendy, chatting about medical school. Background music: Abba songs.

Passing Barrie, Tom and Beth try to engage in conversation. Nothing happens. Both are silent.

Tom, listening to some soft classical music on the radio, tries to engage Beth in conversation. Beth is somewhere else. Beth is looking out of the front window staring at the road lines on the right side. Tom turns his head to the right, "Beth, where are you?"

Beth does not respond. Tom tries again.

"Beth, where are you?"

Beth turns her head toward Tom.

Tom says, "I hope to get a new contract with overseas pearl manufacturers. If I get it, I want to take Rick with me to south of France in late July. The trip will be for about 4 or 5 days. Do you have any objections?"

Beth does not respond.

"We should have good weather this weekend," says Tom. Beth remains silent.

"Can we try to be a bit more friendly?" says Tom. Beth remains silent.

"Beth, are you listening? Are you talking?"

"What's going on?"

Tom and Beth have had their moments in their marriage. Tom kept his eyes on the road remembering the numerous arguments they had about raising the kids.

"Give them more," says Beth.

"No," says Tom.

Invariably, the kids got their way, and Tom and Beth silenced themselves on many issues that continued to divide them. They were no longer compatible. Each was going his or her way.

Beth was staring out the front window. She didn't hear Tom. She was locked into the past much the same way Tom recalled their arguments over the kids, over the in-laws, over which school they should go to, almost over anything.

Beth was burned out. Beth was depressed. Beth was reaching middle age and was pre-menopausal. Her kids were grown up. They no longer needed her for food, shelter, and clothing, just money and laundry. The kids were no longer kids. They did what they wanted to do. They didn't ask for permission. They just did it. The kids were no longer dependent on their parents for their ideas and opinions.

Beth had few friends. Beth had no real hobbies. Beth was no longer interested in a marital relationship. Beth was lost in oblivion. Beth needed help. But she didn't know where to go for it.

One of the Committee Members stands up. "Mr. Gonsalus. I don't wish to interrupt you on this sad story, but where are you going? We all know about these situations."

"Please be patient. This story is not a soap opera or one made for TV. This is a real story, one that deserves your attention. Please bear with me. If I may, I will continue."

Switching cars, Wendy and Melissa traded quips. Both were in medical school, although Melissa was one year away from graduating. They talked about the courses and classmates when Wendy brought up the conversation about Melissa's relationship with Rick. Rick and Melissa were dating, but the relationship was not going anywhere according to Melissa until she graduated and got a job, and then, she didn't know about Rick.

Melissa was having fun, but she was not ready to make a commitment. Their relationship was on and off for the last 6 months, but on this weekend it was on.

Rick, on the other hand, was now working with Tom with a view to learning the advertising business. The business was a small advertising business where Tom and his crew would make still photographs for newspapers and magazines and periodically commercials for television. Tom rented a large warehouse studio in the Toronto downtown east end.

On arriving at Whispering Pines in Muskoka, the Richardson's retreat from the concrete jungle of the Toronto core, Tom and Beth begin unloading the groceries, the flowers, overnight bags, and new treasures for their resort-like home. Rick, Wendy, and Melissa roll in minutes later, to pick up the balance of parcels and carry them inside the home.

While Tom and Beth unpack the groceries from the coolers, Rick and Wendy run down to the dock, open up the boat house, do a quick change into bathing suit bottoms, and dive into the lake one after the other. Melissa from the top of the hill, smiling, laughing, and giggling, yells to Wendy, as she is running down to the boat house.

"Where are you going?"

"We're swimming out to the raft. Come on and join us."

"I can't right now. My bathing suit is in my bag."

"Go get it," says Wendy.

"We'll wait for you on the raft."

"OK, be back in seconds."

On entering the Pines, Tom and Beth are arguing again about having a cozy weekend with their kids and friends, and there may be some cuddling. Their marriage was breaking down.

Throughout the week, Tom works twelve-hour days, only to fall asleep watching the nightly 11 o'clock news, while Beth, at the beginning stages of her menopause, and is having mood swings with the result that she rejects Tom on a regular basis. Beth began to suffer hot flashes, mood swings. She had difficulty sleeping through the night.

While Tom did not physically abuse her, his threatening overtones and banging his fist against the wall were well documented in the marriage breakdown. They yelled at each other with threatening gestures. But there were constant overtones of mental and psychological abuse for the last years.

Beth was regularly traumatized as a result of the ongoing abuse. She didn't know what to do. She didn't know where to go. They were losing faith in each other; they were becoming less compatible; they were no longer having laughs together. Their interests were diverse with only the Muskoka cottage and Toronto home having common links to their marriage.

Beth thinks back to those unhappy events raising children and arguing with Tom much of the time over whether one of the kids should be able to stay up until 11 in evening. Beth always took the lenient side of things. She would tell Tom, Rick has done his homework, so he should be able to stay up late. On the other hand, Tom would counter that Rick was still a young boy and needed extra sleep. Back and forth they went with Rick and Wendy listening from the second level of the home.

"Hello, everyone. Is there anyone here?" asks Melissa, feigning that she does not hear them argue. She hears Tom and Beth talking about their marriage as though it were a pot about to boil over onto the stove.

"Hello, everyone. It's Melissa. Is it all right if we go for a boat ride?"

"Sure," says Beth, "take Rick and Wendy with you. Make sure that there are life jackets in the boat."

Melissa exits minutes later in her one-piece bathing suit, baseball hat, and top cover-up. Tom catches a view from the bay window for seconds of her running down to dock, removing her hat and cover-up, stretching every which way, and then jumping from front of dock into the lake. Melissa performing a head-up crawl approaches the raft. Tom disappears into never-never land while Beth continues to argue about their life together.

"We must have more together," says Tom.

"More what," says Beth.

Tom replies. "We must start enjoying this place again. Or, let's sell it and move on. I need more attention from you. You must see another doctor if your GP is not prescribing the right drugs. Why don't you try some naturopathic medicines? It's all I hear about in the offices downtown."

"Denise Goldbloom is a good physician. We grew up together. She went to medical school, and I became a housewife. I gave up my chance to continue school. That's the past. Stop hounding me!"

"Denise told me to avoid caffeinated drinks such as coffee, some teas, and alcohol. These drinks tended to heat up my body. She prescribed a Mediterranean diet which we have been trying to keep for months."

"What are you looking at?" Tom took out the binoculars from the shelf in the living room and has focused on the raft.

"Nothing," says Tom. "I'm checking out the kids, and the distant neighbors."

Indeed, Tom is glued to the binoculars. He sees Rick and Wendy lying on the raft, bellies down, while Melissa is climbing up the ladder. Tom's heart stops. Melissa opens up her suit from side to side and then the bottom to let the water drain out, her long hair, straight down her back past her shoulders. She bends over, front to back, back to front to back, side to side. Tom is mesmerized.

Melissa climbs over Wendy's back and sits on Rick's bum. She then leans over and starts to massage Rick's back. She moves backward massaging his lower back onto his bum.

Rick says, "Wow. Don't stop. I want to turn onto my back."

Melissa on her knees gently lifts herself up while Rick turns over. Melissa then sits down again on Rick's upper thighs.

Melissa starts to rub Rick's chest while Rick moves his hands to slide Melissa's straps over her shoulders. Rick is about to put his hands on her chest when Wendy perks up and says, "Not here. Save it for your bedroom."

Rick says to Wendy, "Look the other way."

"What do you mean? Look the other way."

"Just do it for 30 seconds."

Wendy rolls over onto her left side.

Rick puts his hands on Melissa's shoulders and then pushes the straps off the shoulders leaving the top part of her bathing suit barely holding up her suit. Melissa sits upright while Rick moves his hands over her breasts while her hands were massaging Rick's abdomen.

Wendy rolls back and then sits up to see what Rick was doing. Rick had a huge grin on his face. Melissa had her hands up and around Rick's neck while Rick was rubbing Melissa's chest with the palms of his hands.

Wendy calls for Rick to stop and yells at Melissa to roll over beside her. Melissa ignores her. Melissa stretches her hands way above her head while Rick moves his head onto Melissa's breasts.

Wendy shouts out, "Stop cooing, both of you. Let's go for a swim."

Tom still glued to his binoculars.

Beth on leaving the kitchen says she'll be back. "I'm going to take a shower."

Tom, still glued, watches Melissa roll over to sit up upright and start playing with Wendy in paddy-cake, paddy-cake game. Both are sitting erect facing each other, laughing smiling, and bantering with each other. By this time, Melissa's top has almost fallen leaving her facing Wendy. This time Rick is rubbing Melissa's back.

Rick and Wendy are 18 months apart, Rick being the older at 25. They have grown up so close, almost as twin brothers and sisters. Rick and Wendy have no inhibitions. While they had separate bedrooms, they each spent lots of time together. They studied together; they dressed together; they danced and sang songs; and they helped each other growing up. He chose her dresses and blouses; she chose Rick's pants and shirts. They were inseparable.

Rick: "I'm going to Cap Ferrat with Dad next month."

"Where's that?" retorts Wendy.

"Southern France, on the Mediterranean Sea. You know, it's where all the better magazine photos are shot. He wants to make a shoot about advertising pearls on the beach for the International Pearl Association of pearl retailers. They gave him a $25,000 expense budget to come up with 3 ads for magazines pushing pearls as being a girls' next best friend after diamonds. The contract is worth over $100,000. You know, pearls are affordable, so get out there and buy some. We'll film some models on the beach displaying strands of pearls."

Wendy: "Is Mom going? She'd love to go to Paris if they are going to stop over."

Rick: "I don't think so. Dad wants to work and then come home. So, I thought I would invite Melissa to come with us. Melissa, do you want to come?"

Melissa: "What! You've got to be kidding. What an invitation! You didn't even ask me."

"I can't get away. We've got two papers due in August. I haven't started yet."

Wendy: "Give me a break. You have lots of time to prepare. You can work on the airplanes while they sleep. When they're working, you can sleep. I have done this before. It works great. Trust me."

Rick: "Well. How about it? Melissa, we'll leave Toronto on a Thursday night, arrive in Paris in the morning and catch the connector to Nice. By noon

Friday, you'll be on the beach sleeping and sun tanning! It's only for a few days."

"Let me think about it. I have to check my calendar to see if I have enough time to research and prepare. Sit back and enjoy the sun."

"Tom, Tom. Come over here. I need you to carry out the boxes," yells Beth coming out of the shower. Tom, still engaged with the binoculars intensely focused on young Melissa, in dreamland, hardly notices Beth who is a few feet away trying to get his attention. Beth, almost naked, with a towel wrapped around her waist and one around her neck, is trying to get Tom's attention.

"Oh, oh," Tom snaps out of it.

"Where have you been?"

"I'm thinking that we're getting too old, too fast. Come on over here. Let's have some hugs and kisses."

"No way, maybe tomorrow."

"How about a massage? You always like a massage after a shower. Let me get started."

Tom approaches Beth, ready and able to give her a hug.

Beth is still as beautiful as in her 20s, but now more than a few pounds heavier. She still looked good to any normal male.

Beth blurts out: "No, no, not now. The kids are around. Some other time."

"You keep pushing me away. C'mon. Let's have some fun."

"The kids are on the raft. There's no one here."

Beth takes the towel and starts to dry her hair. Standing half naked and while drying her hair, Beth gestures to Tom.

"Take the boxes out, Tom," she cuts him off quickly. Tom is in partial shock. He's been rejected, again. He focuses on Beth, but Beth does not see his stare. Instead, he refocuses on Melissa.

Beth hasn't been herself in months, maybe even the last year or so. She's been changing. Estrogen, you know. She doesn't want to take pills or even herbal remedies. She had been experimenting with black cohosh to reduce the daily hot flashes, but that didn't seem to help.

Tom knew his marriage was breaking down. They were putting in time; they were no longer the lovers of twenty years ago; they were no longer compatible with what they wanted in their leisure. Beth was content to golf and play bridge with her cronies, and he was frustrated with her lack of physical attention to him.

They were falling apart as a couple. Love and respect were fading; the marriage was more business-like with little dividends that made them happy. Toleration, that's what they had for each.

Compromise, giving in so there would be no arguments, especially in front of the kids. Heaven forbid!

Beth rarely smiled; Tom rarely laughed. Where were they going?

They were headed for divorce court. That is a federal matter under our Constitution.

First, the separation. Where does Beth go? Does she remain in the home? Does she find a woman's shelter? Was she physically safe? Does she call 911 if he threatens her?

How does Beth protect herself? Beth had no skills. Beth couldn't get a job of any substance. Beth had no independent money to keep her in a modest style pending a support order.

Many women are traumatized by the reality, as a result of the past and ongoing abuses. Breaking up is hard to do.

Tom, still mesmerized by the activity on the raft while Beth reminded herself that she was so unhappy with Tom's treatment.

The emotional abuse was accelerating. At almost every opportunity, Tom would take advantage of Beth. He would mock her in front of Rick and Wendy to the point where Rick and Wendy would intervene.

"Enough. Maybe, it's time for you two to split. We don't want to hear this anymore. Dad, can you do that?"

Tom didn't answer. But he was now thinking about it.

Once lawyers are involved, there is continued abuse by the very fact that they have to see lawyers. The more the parties fight the more the lawyers earn. Then there is legal bullying. One lawyer threatens the other; standoff and more time passes without resolution.

If Beth hires an aggressive family law lawyer, and Tom does the same, there is a tendency to bully each other to a point where one side yields or is worn down to a point that they make a poor compromise. Mediation is the way to go, but many family partners still feel that the lawyers are not doing their job and are capitulating to savvy mediators who also make a good living bringing the parties together.

Legal bullying involves one lawyer bringing motions all the time to cause the other side to surrender or make a 'bad' deal. Courts generally permit the parties to litigate without any one court or judge 'refereeing' the dispute or 'regulating' the bullying.

That's the system. No one has the control or power. Cases get bounced from one court to another without any coordination at all. Only the last hearing that counts, may be; that is the hearing where the judge does rule, one way or the other. And then, there are the appeals. It never seems to end.

Beth had sufficient income where she does not qualify for Legal Aid in Ontario, but enough income to pick the lawyer of her choice. Should Beth have access to any lawyer of her choosing? The lawyers are not all the same; some are better than others; and some charge more than the regular family law lawyer. Some charge a lot, but perform poorly; some charge average rates, but get average results. Some young lawyers don't care what they charge. They just want to win. But at what cost?

Chapter Two
Business Film Laboratory

Tom and Andy

Back in Toronto, Tom and Andy were best friends since 6 years of age. They lived close-by; down the street, a block and a half away. Together, they went through West Preparatory Public school, Forest Hill Collegiate High School, and York University. They were inseparable. In junior high school, they joined the photography club.

The club had a photography room on the third floor where Mr. Clavert, the science teacher, organized and managed the club on Mondays, Wednesdays, and Fridays after school. Mr. Clavert was a tall, skinny man, with black waving hair, slightly gray in the temples. He wore black framed glasses. He had been at the school for many years and was noted as being super-strict not only in the classroom but also in teaching the hobby class on how to use the chemicals.

In all his years teaching, he had a perfect record of not one little accident, not even little one, and he was not about to incur one when Tom and Andy joined. In fact, once he found out about Tom and Andy's talents, Mr. Clavert promoted them to the school staff to record the photos for posterity.

They became master photographers by 15 years and in grade 10, and ultimately for the next 3 years, they were the school's official photographers for the weekly newsletter. They were the official photographers for the school events, sports games, and the annual school yearbook.

Long before digital cameras and technology, Tom and Andy first experimented with taking black and white photos and then developing them in the Tom's basement. Fortunately, Tom's mother let him take a corner storage room and re-vamp it into a photographer's dark room or developing room. It had a huge table beside a deep laundry tub where Tom set out his developers. Tom's mother would peek in now and then to see what they were doing.

Tom's dad gave Tom a Leica camera when he was 7 years old. Tom would go around the house, the backyard, the neighbor's backyard, and down the street shooting one photograph after another. He took photos of his mother washing the dishes, folding the laundry, and getting dressed. He took photos of his dad sitting at the desk working and his dad sitting on the toilet. He would shoot 2 or 3 rolls of 24 shots a day. He then gave them to his dad to take the local photography store for developing.

At first, the developing costs were $1.00 a photo and after several weeks, and many dollars later, Tom's dad said, "No more."

This hobby is costing too much. So, Tom's dad bought Tom basic books on developing film. After reading them over and over, Tom finally persuaded his dad to purchase the tanks, the chemicals, the dark red-light bulb, and even an enlarger. Tom was hooked by 10. His dad seeing the quality of his work, bought Tom more cameras, a Minolta, a Sony, a Voigtlander. Tom's photography was incredible for his age. He had arrived before his time. His future was secure.

Andy was no different. His mom and dad bought him first a movie film camera. Developing film was a challenge, but with Tom at his side, his film became increasingly clearer. Then Andy's dad bought him an original Panasonic video camera by 9. And Andy too went up and down the street shooting everything in sight.

Tom and Andy would cover the school's events. They would attend all the sporting events in which the school participated, football, hockey, basketball, and track events were the most popular.

Andy used to come over after school to develop the film and then hang up the prints on a make-shift close line. They experimented with the chemicals, sometimes the photos were over-exposed; other times under-exposed.

But once they got the right proportions, the photos were as good as any photo-finishing camera store. Girls in the club often hooked up with Tom and Andy mimicking their style. They too would travel with Tom and Andy, and sometimes ended up in Andy's dark room developing film. They experimented with all shades of black and white and of light and dark.

Desperate for objects and people to photos, they took self-portraits and portraits of each other, fruit platters, bookshelves, and tools in the dark room. On occasion, they would invite their classroom girls to come and watch them develop the film.

On occasion, Tom would coach them to model, making funny faces, funny gestures, and funny poses. Andy would photoshoot the girls as they watched Tom take photos of all of them. The lights were low, so taking photos one minute and developing them next was a challenge—and then rewarding when they saw the final product.

On one occasion, Tom and Andy invited Cindy, a classmate, over to Tom's home. Tom gave Cindy one of his cameras and invited her to start shooting. The film was black and white. So, there was no concern about the cost.

First, in the backyard, Cindy started shooting the flowers, the bushes, and then she turned the camera on Tom and Andy. Tom started making funny faces, and made a few sexy poses, flexing his mussels and opening his shirt. Cindy goaded Tom to take off his shirt, and before he was aware, Tom was laughing in his boxer shorts!

Cindy took some more photos when the film ran out. Off to the darkroom to develop the film. Tom closed the door, turned on the red light, opened the camera to retrieve the film. Andy then started to lay out the 3 trays of chemicals needed for the developing.

"Wow," said Cindy. "Look how fast this develops."

Tom still in his boxer shorts said, "It's that simple when you know what you are doing."

Cindy was hooked. She was now part of the photography club.

On one occasion, Tom and Andy invited Cindy back. They took some photos of each other and Tom would then dare her to remove her blouse and in doing so, he would take off his shirt. Nothing new to Cindy as Tom had stripped before. Cindy was at ease with Tom's laisse-faire attitude. Tom would tease her to take her top off.

Andy stood by for the photos. Tom promised her that he would destroy the photos once they were developed. Tom first removed his jersey, and then Cindy gestured that she was not going to do the same. After some more teasing, Cindy lowered her head and then in seconds lifted her jersey top over her head.

"There, there," said Tom. "Nothing too risky. Just pretend you're at the beach or in a swimming pool. You're still wearing a top."

"OK," said Cindy. "What's next?"

"Nothing," said Tom. "Let's take more photos of ourselves. Here, start shooting."

Tom, still in his boxer shorts, made all sorts of moves and gestures. Cindy stopped shooting once the last shot came to an end.

"OK, your turn," said Tom. And Cindy started gesturing while Tom started shooting.

"OK, stop," said Tom. "Let's try to take some photos together. Andy, set up the tripod. I can put the camera on it with a delayed shooting. Here, let me do it."

Once Tom set it up, he gestured Cindy to come over and stand beside him. Together they would hold hands, hold arms, and even in one shot, in a body-to-body hugging position. The photos turned out great. Tom was pleased with the quality and the subject matter, although he was a bit risky, at 15, to encourage Cindy to remove her top.

Cindy was comfortable with Tom. Cindy was now part of the photography club. While they never made a pass for each other, they were attracted. Cindy would then invite her girl friends over to see what Tom was doing.

Tom's skills improved. On a weekly basis, Tom would ask Cindy to come over. Cindy was becoming comfortable in the dark room, taking photos of each other and then developing them. On one occasion, Tom invited Cindy to model in a bathing suit, first in a one piece and then in bikinis. Nothing to it. Cindy would bring over a couple of bathing suits to model in. A bathroom was nearby for Cindy to change. She first put on a one-piece suit. Came out and modeled around the room.

"How do you like it?" says Cindy.

"Great. Keep moving and then hold for a few seconds."

"OK," says Cindy.

"Enough, let's see you in a bikini."

"I have two. Which one do you like?"

"That one," pointing to the one that had less material.

"OK, I'll be back in a minute."

"Wow! Don't you look great!"

Cindy blushed.

And then, Tom gestured her to remove her top. Cindy paused. And then put her head down.

"Cindy, it's just you and me. Don't you want to see what you really look like in a photo?"

Tom went over to her, moved behind, and unhook the top. Cindy turned around and the topic dropped to the floor.

"This is the shot I wanted. You look fantastic!"

They would stand together, both topless, making faces. Tom had a remote button that he could push and then snap away. Cindy was no longer a girl but was young woman with a great figure.

On occasion, Cindy would bring a friend or two to see the setup. Cindy, now comfortable with Tom, would remove her top, make funny poses for Tom to shoot. On one occasion, Tom took off his shirt and beckoned Cindy to do the same. At first, they dared each other, laughed a lot, and then with the lights dim, tops would come off under 'you go first' to giggles of laughter.

Seeing Cindy topless, the other girls followed first with some hesitancy, but later with confidence. No sooner than shooting a roll of film, some 20 or 30 shots in less than 15 minutes, Tom would signal her to gather around the developer to see what came out. Disappointed in the photoshoot and the finished product, they would start round two of 'you go first'.

Tom and Andy were discrete. They destroyed all the photos so Cindy felt safe in coming to Tom's home. The photographs became better and better until the girls were no longer girls, but young women posing for magazines.

And, that's how they got the job of co-photographers at their high school.

****

Beth

Beth had a similar background. She grew up on the other side of the public school. Beth was a couple of years younger than Tom. They did not meet him until they were in the same junior high school, but 2 years apart. Beth was in grade 7 when Tom was in grade 9. Beth was an all-round student and athlete.

At 10, Beth was so photogenic that she appeared in young girls' advertisements as a model holding ketchup, an apron, breakfast cereals, dolls, whatever. Beth's parents were making good money for Beth's education and future life as a model. But Beth had other plans.

At a volleyball practice in grade 7, Beth excelled as the team captain. On the floor with 3 other girls, Beth would serve up the ball and bat it over the net. The volley with the opposing team would go back and forth for several rounds when Beth's teammate set the ball up for a spike.

And wow, Beth punched that ball so hard the other side didn't have a chance to recover. All the while, Tom clicked away with his camera catching Beth in all sorts of poses that makes an editor's job so easy in picking one or two photos for the school's newsletter. And that's when Tom asked Beth over to his house to develop the film. Beth at first said no, but then said maybe later.

And then curiosity got to her. She accepted after several more invitations. She wanted to see his dark room.

Somewhat skittish, somewhat shy, she closed the door to the dark room behind her. Tom gently asked her to sit on one of the chairs overlooking the chemical trays.

"Just watch," he said. "You will see your photos from the volleyball game in tray 3. Once I take them out, I can hang them on the line just above your head. In meantime, let's make a trick photo. Do you mind? It will take a few minutes, but I guarantee that you won't stop laughing."

Beth paused, and then said, "What do you have in mind?"

"Nothing risqué," said Tom.

"OK," she said. "Let's do it."

Tom said he wanted her to put hands up in the air and pretend that she was holding a huge volleyball. While the film was developing, they stepped out of the dark room. Beth held her hands up high; "higher," he said.

Beth had a huge grin on her face smiling as wide as she could, not knowing what was next. As she stretched, Beth's posture changed slightly. She was 19 maturing into a young woman with curves around her chest and curves around her hips. Tom meanwhile was snapping away. Seconds later, he asked to lower her hands and hold a volleyball out in front so that he could photograph the ball.

"Oh, I get it. You want to join the two photographs so that it looks like I am holding up this massive ball. That's neat. Let's do it."

Back in the darkroom, Beth's photos from the volleyball practice were developed and now hanging from the clothesline. Except for the dark red light, they could barely see each other. When Beth looked at the photos, she was ecstatic. They were great photos. So much so, she leaned over to Tom and gave him a huge hug and kiss on his cheek. Tom knew then. Beth was going to be his girlfriend for years.

In return, Beth asked Tom to give her the camera so that she could take shots of Tom. Tom loaded the camera and gave it to her. She began shooting

Tom in all sorts of poses, smiling, laughing, hands up in the air, turned sideways. Tom suggested that they put the camera on a tripod so that they both could be in the photo. The camera had a time delay of about 10 seconds.

Once set up, Beth pushed the camera button and moved over to be beside Tom, both looking into the camera lens. They took several shots with the last shot where Beth kissed Tom. The kiss lasted more than a couple of seconds. As the kiss became more intense, Beth put her hands around Tom's neck. Tom then moved his hands from her shoulders down to her bum. Tom was reserved. He was respectful of Beth, nor did Beth become aggressive toward him.

Unknown to her, Tom was to marry Beth by the time she was 20.

Warehouse Scene

Tom had been in the advertising business for years. On graduating from university, he went to work for Brody & Co., a well-known marketing company. After several years of watching production, Tom decided to uproot and set up his own business.

At first, the business was slow, but Tom persisted in walking up and down streets and offering his services to local merchants. His fees were low compared to the numbers he saw at Brody & Co. He charged his direct expenses for a customer plus a 20% overhead as a loss leader. He went down the street and walked into the flower store, the shoe store, the local coffee shop, and a lot of other neighborhood stores.

From his garage, Tom made brochures for their businesses. He made posters that they could affix to the window. He made window displays of just about everything. Business soon began to grow. The price was right. Local shop owners took advantage of a good thing.

But it paid off. Tom was starting to attract the larger stores and banks as customers. He kept his prices low for the local merchant, but then added another amount for the larger and more lucrative businesses. With profit in hand, Tom was ready to move from his garage to larger premises.

After several years in cramped corners, Tom moved his business into a 30,000-square-foot warehouse, east of downtown Toronto. Tom had a 10-year lease with options to renew for many years. Tom had the warehouse subdivided into 10 small studios with open fronts so that cameras could move along from one set to another. Each studio had its own setup depending upon the type of business he was marketing. Most businesses wanted still photography. Some wanted a 10 to 30 second video commercial.

Tom's business was successful. But he paid a price. He worked day and night only to come home, eat dinner and go to sleep. His kids grew up without much input from Tom. On the other hand, Beth had established ladies' groups to play bridge, canasta, and the odd golf game. They were like two ships passing in the night.

Tom wanted protection for his business. He took advice from his lawyer if the business ran into financial difficulties. Tom took some risks. He moved the business in the early stages from his garage to a large warehouse. He set up a company to hold the lease. However, Tom had to guarantee the landlord.

The business, however, was in a different company. So, his lawyer set up a separate trust to hold the company shares. Andy, his long-time best friend, was the trustee, and Tom, of course, was the beneficiary and recipient of weekly draws and payment of expenses.

Tom now had about 30 employees, many of whom were graduates of advertising from the George Brown Community College. There were makeup artists, photographers, set designers, film developers, carpenters, and door-to-door marketers.

Tom would have between 2 and 4 persons on a project. About 3 employees worked in the office, bookkeeping the costs and expenses, and soliciting new clients. Rick's office was at one end of the building and Tom's at the other. Each morning on arrival, Tom and Rick would walk down the aisle looking at the production in each of the seven studios.

In studio one, Tom was promoting a dry breakfast cereal. In studio two, there were displays of body lotion. In studio three, he was promoting toys and so on.

One studio caught Rick's attention. In studio six, Cato, the manufacturer of handbags, shoes, and scarves, had engaged Tom to come up with a poster promoting their products. Tom retained a model agency to send a woman model. There she was, dressed in the skimpiest outfit to model the handbags, shoes and scarves. As they stopped in front of studio six, the employees were strategically placing the handbags and scarves on the model.

Rick, fresh out of school, was beginning to learn the business. He was amazed to see, hands-on, his father's skill in setting up a scene for the promotion of a product or service.

Rick was excited. He was travelling to the south of France to assist his father in a photoshoot displaying pearls. He couldn't wait. And now that he asked Melissa to come with him, he was doubly excited about travelling to southern France with his girlfriend.

Supreme Coffee Shop

Beth called Joyce Crothers, one of her friends who was a real estate agent and who was the agent that sold Beth's parent's home. Joyce worked for and was part owner of Village Hill Realty Inc., a local franchise operation with multiple locations across Ontario.

Beth and Joyce grew up together in Village Hill, community suburb outside Toronto. Beth went on to be a wife, a homemaker, and mother after university whereas Joyce employed housekeepers while having a family and became interested in selling real estate. Village Hill had several connections with lawyers, lawyers who dealt primarily with real estate, but some were part of a larger firm where family law legal services were provided.

Beth and Joyce met at the Supreme Coffee shop. After about 15 minutes of catching up on what's going on in Joyce's life, then, and then in Beth's life, Beth opened up and confided in Joyce about her marriage being on the rocks.

Joyce's face turned from a smiling blushing face to an almost stoned-faced when she heard Beth tell of moments of mental and emotional abuse from Tom. Beth recounted the number of times that Tom had pushed himself onto her when Beth was neither ready nor willing. Beth said she cried a lot, but without resolution.

Joyce interrupted, "Did he physically hurt you? Did he hit you?"

"No, Tom never hit me as such."

"Carry on, Beth."

"It's not like that," Beth said. "Tom would harass me. He would belittle me. He would mock me. He would verbally put me down in front of the children, and on occasion when we were out with another couple."

"Do you remember last fall when we double-dated at the Primavera Restaurant? I wanted a glass of white wine. When the server approached the table, I asked what was available. When I chose the chardonnay, Tom abruptly told the server to cancel the order. 'She's had enough liquor tonight. One martini too much.' I was embarrassed. You remember that, don't you?"

It was a good thing that Beth confided in Joyce. Beth needed to tell someone who she could trust. She was embarrassed to tell Wendy and Rick, although they may have suspected that their parent's marriage had its ups and downs, and at this time, it was down.

Joyce interrupted again, "Are you safe?"

"Do you think that he will hit you? Do you know how to protect yourself?"

"No, none of that. But he's wearing me down. I've tried to talk to him about our marriage, but it seems that we are in different worlds now and have been for the last few years. He is busy at work and doesn't play golf anymore. He sees these young women models at the warehouse, but as far as I know, he has remained faithful. At this stage, I really don't care. I need some resolution even if that means getting a divorce."

"I think you should protect yourself. You don't know what's ahead, but you can be assured that it's not going to be nice and friendly."

"What are you suggesting?"

"Take copies of all his income tax returns, bank books, passports, health cards, and investments. You're going to need these for your lawyer and accountant."

Joyce was priming Beth for the worst. Like Joyce should know. Joyce had been married three times. The first time she married for love. She was young, beautiful, and totally naive. After 2 years of marriage, she got burned by the divorce. Her husband's lawyers outmaneuvered her lawyers.

The second time Joyce was prepared. She knew that divorce was big business to law firms where one spouse had money and assets. While Joyce loved each husband, she wasn't ready when the time came for the husbands to look for younger women.

Joyce obtained a pre-nuptial agreement from her second husband without a hassle. Little did she know that his business was about to fail, and with that, his personal assets were in jeopardy. That marriage ended when the bankruptcy trustee came with a moving crew to empty the home.

Joyce was happily married now, but she was more realistic in knowing marriages were not made in heaven nor were there marriages made for life. Joyce was better prepared for husband number 3. This time she insisted on seeing bank accounts and tax returns.

Change of Plans

Manny Eras was summoned to Tom's office. Tom had received a telephone call from 'Cottage Country', a monthly publication of stories and articles on 'how to' and 'what if' subjects. The publisher of Cottage Country was looking for new consultants to display advertisements and articles in their magazine.

Manny was a natural for this assignment. While Manny had been in Tom's employment for over 15 years, and by this time, he had a percentage of profits, he usually ran the shop from the inside. However, in this case, Manny Eras grew up in Parry Sound, knew almost all the merchants and many cottagers in the area. Tom thought Manny was perfect for the assignment.

Manny's background gave him a definite advantage over Tom or anyone else in the shop. After half an hour discussing the approach and speaking to Cottage Country, both agreed that Tom would carry on with his trip to Cap Ferrat, that Manny would spend the week in Parry Sound, Huntsville, and Port Carling, and that Tom would speak to Rick about staying in Toronto to mind the shop.

Tom knew that Rick would be upset, but this was an opportunity for Rick to monitor the various photoshoots, coordinate rehearsals, answer client concerns, and manage the payroll. Tom had been showing Rick various aspects of the business and two years ago gave him cheque-signing authority at the bank. Rick was taking over the business every time Tom absented himself from Toronto. Each time, Rick assumed more control, and with Manny's help, caused to manage the business in a profitable and efficient manner.

Rick had waited for the golden opportunity to manage the shop. So, it was left to Tom to tell Rick that he should stay in Toronto and that when the next foreign assignment comes along, that he would be going, for sure.

Rick wanted desperately to manage the shop, but he was also equally craving the trip to Cap Ferrat. He helped plan the trip and knew all the details.

Rick had travelled with Tom on several assignments over the years, but those took place when he was much younger, and tagged along for the sites, good food, and souvenirs. Then, Rick was oblivious to what Tom was doing, but subconsciously, Rick could have performed the assignment, much like Tom, the only difference being that he was somewhere between 10 and 18 years old, and no model or business person would have given him the respect he wanted. So, Rick was ready to go on this trip more than ever.

Tom broke the news. He told Rick that there was a change of plans. Rick was disappointed, to say the least. But he knew that this was his opportunity to manage the advertising business while Manny was in Muskoka and Tom overseas. Melissa had the choice of staying back or joining Tom overseas. At Rick's encouragement, Melissa decided to spend the time overseas and enjoy the sites.

Tom and Rick organized the trip to Cap Ferrat. Tom used his agent Fred Zimmer who was part of an international photographers association. Tom and Fred met several years earlier at a convention in Orlando and maintained contact throughout the years. Now, it was an opportunity for the two to work together as Fred was a well-known photographer for some of the magazines in France. He was resident in Nice, and Cap Ferrat was a short motor drive away. Tom left the details to Rick.

For weeks before the trip, Rick and Fred organized the shoot. Rick booked the airflights through Paris to Nice, rental car on arrival in Nice, and two adjoining rooms in a pensione in Cap Ferrat that was highly recommended by Fred. The rooms overlooked the Mediterranean Sea. They were within a short walking distance to the beach down a pebble stone walkway with stores and restaurants. Fred emailed photos of the rooms showing the view of the sea from their private balconies.

Rick and Fred retained 3 professional models, one black, 5 feet, 8 inches, 120 pounds, 21 years old with long black hair that draped over her shoulders. By anyone's imagination, she was gorgeous and had been in the modeling business for just over 3 years in Nice. The model had been the subject matter of several glossy European magazines modeling everything from shampoo, earrings, to evening dresses. As they say, soup to nuts. Unknown in North America, this was her opportunity to break into the marketplace.

Consequently, Fred negotiated a favourable contract with her agency that fit within the budget for the shoot. The two other models were just as beautiful. One came from Corsica, slightly shorter, but still had the lean and mean look that models often display. She was Mediterranean in complexion and colour, with dark brown eyes and dark brown hair. The other model came from Genoa.

She had a Nordic complexion, blue eyes and blonde hair. She had an hourglass figure. Fred couldn't ask for anything more. Three beautiful girls who would display these genuine pearls for all women of different sizes and shapes, colours, and ages. Fred had made arrangements for these models to come to Cap Ferrat the day before the shoot was to take place.

The International Pearl Association wanted to make pearls as popular as diamonds are forever. That was the assignment. 'Pearls to the End of Time'.

That was the task and one that would take more than one shoot, one set of advertisements, and more than one year to become popular. Both Tom and Manny knew the size of the assignment. This was their beginning into the big leagues of advertising.

In this shoot, Tom, Rick, and Fred designed the layout meticulously. Tom supervised while Rick and Fred supplied the detail and the sets needed for the shoot. One model was to wear pear earrings and a 3-strand necklace, and the other two models, two earrings and pendants. As the final photographs were to be placed in European markets, the model had to appear topless with bikini bottoms. Tom wanted eye-catchers. As for the North American market, the models had to wear bikini tops.

The International Pearl Association wanted a splash in both markets, and so, Tom, Fred, and Rick wanted the page to be memorable and talked about in men's and women's circles, the object of the advertisement to sell pearls to your friend, lover, or partner. The European market was opening up to new displays of jewelry. While rings and watches dominated the marketplace, there seemed to be room for a 'strand of pearls'.

And there were all kinds of pearls. White pearls, black pearls, gray pearls, silver pearls, iridescent pearls, and red pearls. Pearls from fresh water and saltwater oysters. Pearls from the Caribbean, China Sea, and Japanese Sea. A pearl was a smooth rounded bead found in the shells of oysters and other mollusks. When strung together, they make a beautiful necklace, bracelet, or pair of earrings.

It was now the time for the International Peal Association to make a splash about pearls to the end of time. The Association had been lobbying for years in the European and North American marketplaces but were consistently overshadowed by the diamond market. Now was the time that new sensitive magazine articles on the benefits of the pearl as jewelry.

Chapter Three
Travel Arrangements

Fred Zimmer had done his job. Fred was Tom's agent in Europe. Each time Tom travelled to Europe, Fred would arrange for a car, hotel, or pension, reservations for a couple of dinners, local models, and support staff.

For this trip, Fred set up the travel arrangements with Rick. Fred had arranged the airline tickets through Air Canada to Paris. Tom and Rick would leave at 9:00 PM and were expected to arrive in Paris, De Gaule airport, early in the morning.

They were to have a short stay there and fly Air France at 9:00 AM to Nice arriving at 1 in the afternoon. At the Nice airport, Fred arranged for a car to meet them and transfer them to Cap Ferrat and then to the pensione. At Cap Ferrat, Fred had a local car rental company arrange for a car. Fred arranged for a local photographer to meet at the pensione.

Tuesday Night

Tom met Melissa at Terminal 1 at the airport at 6:30 in the evening. Each took their own limo to the airport with arrangements to meet at the Air Canada international check-in counter. They were flying Air Canada to Paris with a connector from Air France in the morning to Nice. Tom and Rick were expected to arrive in Paris early in the morning and fly to Nice arriving at 1 in the afternoon.

They would have dinner, a couple of glasses of wine, and hopefully some sleep. Fred knew the schedule and would be on hand to pick them up at the airport. Fred was initially expecting Tom and his son, Rick. But a few days ago, Tom emailed Fred to arrange for an adjoining room at the pensione. Tom told him that Rick's girlfriend was coming over as Rick had to stay in Toronto to manage the business.

Tom and Melissa checked in together and proceeded through security to gate number 2087. Each had a carry-on bag that fits in the overhead. This was convenient as they did not have to check in baggage. Tom's case, however, was loaded with photography equipment, and minimal clothes. They had an hour on their hands, so Tom suggested that they proceed to local bar for a glass of wine.

Melissa was apprehensive. There she was at the last-minute travelling to Cap Ferrat with her boyfriend's father. She didn't know what to expect, except a great short holiday in the south of France. Tom on the other hand didn't think much of it.

If anything, Melissa's coming was a bonus for Tom as he would be alone for most of the time and she would provide company for him. Tom was the perfect host and gentleman. He thought that Melissa would provide some sort of diversion for him during the slack time of setting up the photography shoot.

Melissa was 26. Tom was 44. Melissa at the bar talked a lot about her upbringing and then meeting Wendy in medical school. Tom showed her two cameras and asked if she was prepared to snap away once the shoot began. Tom reviewed the cameras with Melissa and showed her how to focus and shoot.

Boarding the airplane at 8:15, they took their seats. Once the airplane took off, they were offered a glass of wine. They both took another glass, and within a few minutes of sipping the wine, Melissa's head dropped off and leaned against Tom's right shoulder.

With Melissa sound asleep, Tom opened up his computer to review the schedule in Cap Ferrat. Tom wanted Fred to know that everything should be timed, and to provide alternatives if there was inclement weather or one of the models suddenly became unavailable. Tom had worked on the layouts for the shoot back in Toronto and reviewed them in detail with Fred. After an hour of reviewing the program, Tom nodded off.

Several hours later, the airplane was circling the De Gaule Paris airport. On arrival, each headed for the washroom to freshen up before boarding the airplane to Nice.

Wednesday Morning

Fred and Tom had not seen each other for a few years. Time had stood still. Neither appeared older, grayer, or paunchier than they last recalled. On greeting each other, Tom introduced Melissa.

"Unfortunately, Rick, could not make it," said Tom. "I know we had been planning this trip for months, but some new business developed a few days before we left. Someone had to stay. And we couldn't postpone this shoot."

"Where does Melissa fit in?" replied Fred.

"She's Rick's girlfriend and she was coming along for the ride."

"Well, I hope you have a good time over the next few days. It's exciting as you will see," said Fred.

Wheeling their carry-on luggage, Tom, Melissa, and Fred headed to the parking lot where Fred's red van was parked. In the back, Fred had stored all the camera equipment and a portable changing hut. There was just enough room for the baggage on the top of the car. It was a warm sunny day around 28 Celsius. All 3 were grinning from cheek to cheek. Fred took off to Cap Ferrat, some 30 plus kilometres from the airport.

On arriving at the pensione at 1 on Wednesday afternoon, Fred met the black model who was waiting in the reception area sipping iced coffee. Tom and Fred had been corresponding with Louis Defret by fax, phone, and email for over 3 months. Louis was the manager of the modeling agency.

Ultimately, after reviewing hundreds of photos, Tom and Fred agreed to hire Cecile, the black model, for 6 hours of modeling time. Tom didn't know if he needed 6 hours for 3 models, but since there was already significant expense involved, he was better safe with the additional time.

After checking into the pensione, Tom told Fred to take Cecile for a walk to the photo site and outline what he expected from her. Tom said he would meet them there in an hour's time, but he wanted to walk down with Melissa.

The beach was about a 10-minute walk down a cobblestone road. Along the road were store after store selling everything from beach wear to hardware and fabrics, and some restaurants. It was a bustling road restricted to pedestrian traffic only. Cars had to go around the road to reach the beach.

But first, Tom and Melissa went upstairs to the third floor in an elevator built for just two persons and carry-on luggage holding their breath. Tom and Melissa inches away from each other had huge grins on their faces when Tom started to sing "Getting to know you, getting to know you" when the elevator stopped.

Melissa exited first with her hand luggage and then Tom. They walked down the hall to Room 33, Tom opened the door and said, "This is your room. The bathroom is over there beside the TV and the clothes cupboard. I'm next door. There is an adjoining room to the right. Let's unpack and take a half-hour nap. Let's see. It's now 2:30. Shall I knock on your door at 3:30?"

Melissa replied, "OK." Tom left.

Beach Wear Shop

Nap time finished. Down to the beach by 4:00 to review the site that Fred had chosen and review the shoot with Cecile. Tom walks with Melissa down to the beach. They are both in shorts and shorts carrying a bolos type of bag on their shoulders. As they approach the waterfront, Tom spots a beachwear shop and gestures Melissa to go into the store. They each look around, and then Tom offers to buy Melissa a new bathing suit.

"No thank you," says Melissa.

"Please try one on."

Melissa reluctantly looks over the rack of women's bathing suits and then points to a one-piece suit. Tom laughs and says, "Try it on."

The bathing suit had a deep 'v' in the front with shoulder straps and an open back.

"While you're trying on that one, here take a few more to try on. Come out and let's take a look."

Melissa took another two one-piece suits when Tom reached over her and gave her 3 bikini outfits.

"No," said Melissa. "I don't often wear bikinis at home. Why should I try one now?"

"Except for me, no one knows you. And quite frankly, no one really cares about what you wear or don't wear as you will see. You're in southern France, not southern Ontario. Relax, at least try one or two on to see if you like it."

Melissa takes the 6 bathing outfits into the dressing room. The shopkeeper, a young 30-plus woman offers to assist Melissa. Being somewhat shy, Melissa declines her assistance. "I'm OK, thank you, merci," says Melissa.

Minutes later, Melissa comes out of the dressing room in the first of the one-piece bathing suits. Tom whistles.

"Great suit. You make it. The designer must have had you in mind when he or she designed it. Turn around; turn around the other way. Can you bend slightly to the left? Yes, that's it."

Tom beckons the shopkeeper for a second approval. The shopkeeper suggests one of the other suits may be better.

"Melissa, try on the other one piece. Let's take another look."

Again, minutes later, Melissa emerges with the second one-piece suit. She turns around and around, smiling from check to check, waiting for Tom or the shopkeeper to give his or her thumbs up. Nothing happened. They liked it, but that was it.

"OK," says Melissa. "I'll try on one of the bikinis."

Again, minutes later, Melissa comes out modeling a bikini outfit. The top was full as though it were a coloured bra. The bottom was loose-fitting underpants. The outfit was not flattering nor complimentary to Melissa. Both the shopkeeper and Tom pointed their thumbs down.

Next, Melissa holds up the next bikini. She says she will not try this one on.

"Look, Tom, there is hardly any material on the top, and barely covers up my chest. And the bottom. It's like a G-string with nothing in the back. I can't wear this. I can't. It's far too skimpy and I'm embarrassed to wear it. No. I can't wear this."

"OK," says Tom. "Try another bikini."

The shopkeeper points to one which she thinks will work. Not too skimpy, but enough material to cover up the essentials.

Melissa emerges again, this time with the perfect bikini. Tom beckons her to turn around and around in modeling the outfit as well as to seduce Tom as to her beauty.

Melissa reminded Tom of Beth 25 years ago in the dark room. Tom then was photographing Beth in her bra and panties, something similar to Melissa's top and bottom. Tom was speechless. He stared at Melissa while Melissa kept calling Tom to speak.

Finally, Tom says to the shopkeeper, "We'll take it. No need to put it in a bag. Melissa, just put your top and shorts on as we head down to the beach."

On leaving the shop, Melissa leans over to thank Tom.

On the beach, now about 4 PM, Tom heads over to the planned location for the shoot tomorrow. Tom takes out a large beach towel from his bag, spreads it on the sand, takes off his jersey top and shorts leaving him with his boxer swimsuit.

"Come on, Melissa. Let's go for a swim."

At this time of the day, many come down to the beach for a short swim in the Mediterranean and then lie out to dry for an hour's sun. The women and girls are mostly topless and the men are in bikini bottoms.

Melissa was not about to go topless, nor was Tom prepared to wear a bikini bottom. Melissa giggled at the sight. Her mouth was open to seeing such an open display of flesh. The beach was far from crowded, but enough people spread out. The heat of the sun was now wanning so there were few umbrellas in the sand.

"Down to the water," beckoned Tom.

Melissa then removed her T-shirt and shorts and ran down to the sea. Splashing each other and then diving into the sea, both came up for air looking at each other. Melissa got Tom's attention when she reached down into the water and picked up a handful of sand and then went over to Tom and when he was looking out into the sea, she quickly dropped the sand down the back of his swimsuit. That did it.

Tom, with a smile on his face, hadn't been attracted to too many women since meeting Beth, did the same. However, he went up to Melissa standing in 3 feet of water washing up on the shore, put his hands around as though he were to kiss her, and then dropped the sand into her bikini bottom. She screamed in a funny sort of way. Aghast, and yet enjoyed bantering with Tom.

"Tit for Tat," says Tom.

Melissa sat down in the water to let the sand out. The bottom was loose enough that she could almost take it off in the water and put it back on without anyone noticing.

Tom then swims out into the sea, submerges, and takes off his trunks to remove the sand from the suit and from his body. Melissa noticing Tom's cleansing his suit heads out in a different direction to do the same. She dives into the sea, removes her bottom, does a quick rinse, and puts it back on.

They leave the sea to lie on the towel to dry off. Tom on his back; Melissa on her front. Twenty minutes later, they both had their time in the sun.

Approaching 5 PM, they bundle up the towel and put on their shorts to head back to the pensione for dinner.

Dinner

Fred had engaged 4 models, Cecile, a model from Corsica, and two from Nice. The two from Nice were from the local agency. They were friends since childhood and become models in their early teens. Fred called the hotel where the Corsican and the other two models were staying. Not one had checked in. Fred was in a panic. He called the agency, but it was after hours. He emailed Rick in Toronto, but Rick had not picked up his email as yet as Fred was 5 hours ahead. Tom and Melissa were in the air flying across the Atlantic.

Fortunately, Fred had their cell telephone numbers. He called the Corsican. She answered.

"Where are you?" Fred said.

"I'm been calling you all night. Your cell is off. I get this recording saying that you are not connected. I'm still in Corsica."

"You're supposed to be here in Cap Ferrat. When can you come?"

"I can't come. There are no planes out today and for the next few days. We had an accident here at the airport and the Civil Aviation Authority is conducting an investigation."

"What about the boat? There are two boats a day."

"I can't get reservations. The port has been flooded with calls for seats. The earliest that I can come is Monday, next week."

"Forget it," said Fred. "Everything is set up for tomorrow. Friday."

Fred didn't have much luck with the models from Nice. They too had been trying to contact Fred by cell to say that they can't come. One of the model's grandmother passed away and she is needed in Nice for the funeral and burial procession. The friend did not want to come alone, so they both had to say no.

"Oh, well," mused Fred. "There's lots of girls on the beach. We can probably save a few dollars, and if we can't get a couple, we can go with our main model, Cecile."

It was too late for Fred to get ahold of the agency or any other agency for two more models.

Fred had performed many such shootings over the years, but this time, he knew he had to produce something significant. Tom, while an excellent photographer, did not have the same expertise nor training to produce the type of work that would put Tom's company at the top of the North American market. Tom needed and relied on Fred for the models, the setup, and of course the photoshoot.

The Shoot—Thursday Morning

Tom, Melissa, and Fred finished breakfast on that Thursday morning by 8:30. Packing up their equipment, in shorts and shorts with bathing suits underneath picked up a taxi outside the pensione/hotel about one kilometre from the location on the beach that they had chosen the day before. Within minutes, they arrived in front of the public beach, exited the taxi, and walked across the boardwalk to the site with all their equipment.

Arriving at the beach setting, Fred began at once to set up his two tripods and 35 mm digital cameras. Fred was a perfectionist. He wanted the sun at the right angle, he wanted the tide hitting the water's edge at different angles and he wanted the backdrop on the beach with people in the distance sunbathing and partly out of focus. He had tested the light and reflection on Wednesday afternoon, but now it was Thursday morning with the light flowing from the opposite direction.

Fred brought a few portable chairs, some blankets, and a cooler filled with cold drinks and some party sandwiches for the periodic breaks. He also brought with him a cosmetic box which he needed for make-up of the models. While Cecile didn't need much make-up, Fred knew that if he found others on the beach, he would have to apply some eyeliners, mascara, rouge, and some blush powder.

With Tom's assistance, Fred began to set up a make-shift changing room. Four 6-foot poles and a batik cotton sheet that was wrapped around the poles fit the bill. Melissa helped Fred place the poles in the sand about 4 feet apart so that they formed a small square on the ground. Simple, efficient, and practical.

Cecile, the black model, was already partly made up. Fred now had to finalize the look and colouring. Fred was fluent in French, Tom and Melissa were not. They could get by with simple high school French and lots of sign language and smiles. Melissa was very excited. She couldn't believe the details of the setup that Tom and Rick had organized.

Cecile went into the changing area, disrobed, and put on her two-piece bikini. Within minutes, she was ready for the final make-up. Fred was nervous. He was missing two models. He kept thinking that Cecile was enough, but he knew that Tom wanted people in the background to form a composite. That's what they designed weeks earlier.

Fred then gave Cecile pearl earrings and the necklace to put on. He then re-arranged how they were hanging on Cecile's ears and neck. Cecile stood still as though she was frozen. She was a professional model used to being set up as a prop.

Melissa started to help. She assisted in arranging Cecil's hair so that the pearl earrings would be visible on the shoot. She made sure that they were secure and that they hung properly. Tom brought these gems from Toronto. They were the finest of pearls. While the setup was taking place, some 30 minutes, Tom was busily taking photos using both his cameras. He, too, was very excited. This could be it. His entry into the biggest market of advertising. The moment had come. The shoot was ready to begin!

But there were two markets to satisfy. Europe where partial nudity was the norm and acceptable, and North America where partial nudity was still not widely accepted. Melissa giggled when Fred face to face with Cecile adjusted the pearl necklace. Cecile didn't flinch. Fred had considerable experience in photographing nudes and was cautious, courteous, and careful in making the adjustment. Tom, standing back, was using his digital camera to review the poses with Fred before Fred used his 35 mm camera.

Tom and Manny had planned the composition several months ago. They wanted to show the pearls from a line just below the eyes to a line just above the belly button or navel partially exposing Cecile's breasts. The focal point would be the necklace or pendant hanging on a model's bare chest. Some of the shots would include a full facial, and then partial facial. Other shots had the lower half of Cecile's face and the upper half of her chest.

Cecile's face was so beautiful, that it was difficult not to include it in the many of the photos. They were there to sell pearls, and so that was the centre of attraction. For North Americans, Cecile was to cover up slightly using her bikini top. Same image, different focal point.

10:30 in the Morning

"OK, Cecile, please take your top off. Let the pearls dangle on your chest."

Melissa gasped. She didn't know the models were going topless. Melissa had an innocent smile on her face. She didn't know the model was going to remove her bikini top. She felt self-conscious, blushed, and put her head down. Tom had told her on the way over that there would be two shoots, one for the North American market, and the other for the European market. He told

Melissa that the European market was used to seeing topless women. Melissa was so excited on the airplane that she forgot almost everything Tom had said.

Cecile standing erect, looking somber, removed her bikini top. Fred gestured Cecile to face the waterfront staring out into the sea. Fred held up his right hand and on stretching it out asked that Cecile focus her eyes on his fingertips.

"Look here, look here," he exclaimed.

Fred knew he needed two more models for the shoot. He counted on the girls on the beach to fill in. He knew by this time that it would be busy but not yet crowded.

The sun had been up for a few hours moving from the east along the beach over the sea. By 11:30, Fred and Tom reckoned that the sun will be in the right place for shots against the backdrop of the town and along the beachfront up looking north from the east. Lighting is everything in photography, even today with all the digital equipment and fast films to capture scenes where the lighting is poor.

Fred zoomed in. He began clicking one photo after another, each one slightly different from the other. A little up, a little to the right, a little to the left. Tom had two digital cameras. He gave one to Melissa, gave her another 60 second review of the buttons, and told her to start shooting. Tom was also shooting with his digital camera. Tom was getting great shots, which Rick would eventually see. Tom wasn't thinking. He wasn't thinking his photos would be sitting on Rick's desk several days later.

The scenery was spectacular. The black model in full sunlight, topless, and wearing cultured pearls was the centre of attraction on the beach. Lots of people gathered around to see the shoot. Something they were used to seeing on the Mediterranean coast. That was it, thought Tom. Tom thought men and women would focus their eyes on the strands of pearls and pearl earrings around beautiful necks. Europeans were accustomed to seeing topless women, so there was no blush in these photos.

Then again, Tom thought that North Americans weren't really ready for this. Showing partial nudity may offend some women's groups, although those standards seem to be changing in North America. To appease both, Tom and Fred intended that Cecile would cover up for the North American market. Fred could do this by airbrushing or simply cutting off the photos in the appropriate places.

That's what Tom and Fred did. First, they took photos without a bikini top and then with a bikini top. Cecile had a beautiful bust, thin waistline, and curvy thighs that were covered with the skimpiest of bottoms.

"It's time for a break," said Tom. "Cecile, why don't you change into something else, and perhaps tie your hair back for a different view."

Fred then asked Melissa to walk down the beach to see if she could find 2 or 3 young women who would come over for 100 USD to stand in the background while the shoot was going on.

"Make sure they're topless," says Fred. "It's the effect we want to show in the photo."

"Sure," says Melissa. "But I can't speak French. Here's two one hundred bills. Show them the money; they'll understand. You have high school French, don't you?"

"Yeah, but how do I say 'topless'?"

"You don't have to say that. Just look for topless girls. They are all over the place. Remember, you're in France. They don't have to be as beautiful as you or Cecile, but they should be tall with a good figure. Like your figure. OK?"

Tom and Fred continued with the setting up of the shoot. They started shooting Cecile from all angles with the sea and land as backdrops. Fred was aware of the scenery in setting up his tripods, looking where the sun was moving and taking light metre tests at each step.

Melissa wandered up the beachfront away from the sun. First, she marched with giant steps with a mission in mind. After the first hundred yards, Melissa tempered her gait but still fervently looking for two or three young women to approach. Being highly selective, she knew that she would have to select two or three from a group of friends.

The beach area was starting to fill up with people of all ages, young and old, and kids everywhere. Almost all the young people wore skimpy bath suits and the girls virtually nothing. The men she starred at tight wore speedo suits, jock-strap like that left little to the imagination. After gawking for a few minutes, she recomposed herself and kept looking for candidates. Nothing she hadn't seen before as a medical student. But somehow, it was different here.

Melissa approached a group of seven or eight young girls. only to be rebuffed when she politely said, "Voulez vous venez avec moi," holding up a US 100 dollar bill in the air. "We're just down there," pointing to Tom, Fred, and Cecile. "We need a couple to be in the background," she said in English, "All you have to do is to stand in the background, smile and look natural. Nothing more. Is that all right?"

The girls laughed, and responded, "Double it and we will come!"

The girls spoke more English than Melissa spoke French.

Melissa had only three hundred dollars, thinking that she would bring back three girls. But these girls were beautiful, in their twenties she thought, and not much younger than she was. So, she decided to pick two and offer them $300. Melissa kept waiving the 3 $100 bills in front of two young girls.

"Come with me. One hour. Une heure. And you can have the 3 $100 bills. What do you say?"

The girls replied in English, "What do we have to do for this?"

"Just stand in the background and look at the camera. Nothing more. Can you do that?"

Well, that's how it happened. She made her pick. "You and you. Here's $300. I'll give you the money after the photoshoot. Come with me, Only one hour, une heure."

The two young women were a picture of beauty and desire.

Minutes later, Melissa saunters down the beach with these two girls, Melanie and Francoise, arm in arm, laughing and giggling. Their tops hanging from the bottoms. Fred looked them over, up and down, front and back, and said, "Fine, trés bien, Melissa. But we could use one more person in the backdrop."

Fred told the girls to sit behind Cecile until he was ready to take photos. The girls sat down talking to each other and patiently waiting for the signal.

Fred hesitated. "Melissa, can you go down the beach again, perhaps the other way, and see if you can find one more person. You should still have $100."

"No, no," said Melissa. "I promised Melanie and Francoise $300. I don't have any more money."

Fred reached into his pocket looking for more money. When he looked at his money clip, he had only 357 US dollars left. He thought he could give Melissa another $150 but then decided against it as he needed more cash money for later.

"Hey, Tom. Do you have any American money?"

"Well," said Fred. "We don't have enough cash left. We'll just have to use the two young women we have in the photoshoot. Maybe you [looking at Melissa] want to be in the shoot?"

"Who, me?" Melissa smiled. Put her head down. "You can't be serious. I don't look like these two girls. They're so beautiful."

"But so are you," said Fred.

Tom looking on said, "Let's get on with the shoot. It's going to be noon soon and this place will be mobbed with people. What's the problem?"

"We only have two girls in the background. I think we need three. Melissa might join. But she said she doesn't want to go topless."

Tom shouted back, "I can't hear you. Tell Melissa to go down the other side and look for another person."

"Well," said Fred. "Are you up for it? You'll have to go topless."

Tom perked up. He overheard Fred ask her to be the third model, but Melissa kept shaking her head no.

Melissa, too, hesitated. "I would like to be in the photoshoot, and perhaps, if the right photo is selected, I would be in the magazine. Can I have more than $150? But I can't go topless."

"No, no," said Tom. "You can't appear topless. Rick would kill me if he saw the photos."

"I could wear a top. Just use the photos for the North American market."

Fred looked at Tom, and Tom at Fred. Both then looked at Melissa, smiled, and then said to her, "Let's see you with these two girls."

"You could wear your top for the North American market."

Melissa discarded her shorts in seconds showing her new bikini briefs.

"Not bad," said Fred. "The lower half looks good. Now for the top."

"No way," said Melissa. "I'm not French. I can't go topless."

Melissa then reached for the bottom of her tank top and then adjusted her bikini top. There she was. Standing in her new white bikini top and bottom, She stretched into the air making an 'x' configuration, Fred blurted out, "You're hired!"

"I'll take you the way you are."

As Tom was lining up Cecile for the direct film shot, Fred summoned the three girls, Melanie, Francoise, and Melissa, to move behind the model. Fred said en francais, "Please put your bikini tops on."

"Over here," said Melissa.

"No, slightly to the left. We want to photograph the model from the water into the mountains on the north side. You girls will be about 20 feet in the background looking at the model with envy. I want to see everyone's teeth. So, smile, please."

"More to the left. Yes, that's it. Now make a V, Melissa, you in the middle, think, the other girls on each side. No, no. Stop yelling, Fred."

Fred began snapping away, Cecile in focus, the girls not so, and vice versa. Both Fred and Tom had, of course, the latest camera equipment. Several cameras in fact. Fred had a 35 mm Leica with a 300mm telephoto lens, other lens down to 25 mm. Fred also had, as did Tom, two new 10-megapixel digital cameras. Of course, the beauty of the digital cameras was to give them an instant, and in many ways, an almost perfect photograph.

Tom too was snapping away, but in minutes, he began to focus his digital camera on the amateurs, not the model. Tom looked at Melissa differently.

Working 12-hour days, Tom was burning the candle at both ends. He was making great inroads for his business, but it was taking its toll. He had less time for his family and when he did meet with them, there were often disappointments and disagreements. Tom's marriage had been waning for the last few years, and it appeared that he was compensating for his love for the business more than his love for his wife.

Beth, too, was passing through the last few years alone and hounded by demons and nightmares, imbalances, and loss of youthfulness.

Tom and Beth were slowly parting company. They were losing the jest of being together. It was a matter of time before the cracks in the marriage became obstacles. They were headed for separation.

Looking for excuses, something was bound to happen to trigger the end of a relationship.

There it was. It was happening on a beach in the Mediterranean. The amateur girls were bantering in French with Melissa, playing in the sand, and making all sorts of poses and noises that appeared to delight both Fred and Tom. Fred now was busy. He was taking several photos a minute from all different angles of the model, most of them waist up and close up to see the sparkle of the pearls on an almost bare-chested black woman.

She was gorgeous. The pearls, an off-white, in three strands, hung gracefully on her neck. They were gorgeous too. Fred's job was to make sure that the photos came out where they suggested to the reader "Buy me, buy me, I'm at the local jewelry store."

Tom kept staring at the girls. They were fixing their bottoms, adjusting their tops, dancing, and singing. Melanie and Francoise then approached Melissa, arms stretched out so as to form a minicircle. They touched Melissa's shoulders resting their hands on top, then moving down to her hips and gesturing that they should huddle up with their arms around each other and one another performing a circular dance.

Fred continued with the shoot while Tom focused on a young bashful and beautiful Melissa. Fred yelled over, "10 more minutes. Melissa, ask the girls to face each other with you in the middle. They should be touching your shoulders."

The French girls put their hands around Melissa's back, body to body.

Fred summoned the girls to remove their tops. Melissa hesitated and withdrew from the formation. They unhooked their tops. Backing off slightly, and within seconds, the French girls signaled Melissa to let the top drop to the sand. Melissa signaled, "No."

Melissa was reluctant, but the girls summoned Melissa to come back and stand in the middle. Melissa put her hands on their shoulders as Melanie unhooked the bikini top. As Melissa leaned over, her top dropped to the ground. Melissa was stunned. There stood three young women shoulder to shoulder. Melissa's head was down. She had a sheepish smile on her face, one of innocence and purity, at least by North American standards, and nothing unusual by European standards.

At first, Melissa raised her head to see who was watching. Tom and Fred. But this was nothing. For them, as photographers, topless women for that matter was their business.

Melissa looked at Tom, the father of his son's girlfriend, almost nude. Tom looked at Melissa through his viewfinder and clicked away. She knew. She knew that Tom was photographing her and only her.

People began gathering around the photoshoot. Curious, they saw these girls modeling around a black woman dressed in 3 strands of pearls. They were looking at Melissa and the other two girls. Melissa was self-conscious.

"All these people looking at me."

Not really, they were looking at the shoot as a whole. Melissa just happened to be one of the models.

Melissa reached down for her top. Melanie and Francoise leaned in front of her and placed their hands on Melissa's back as if to say it's OK. Melissa stood up with her top in hand carefully covering her breasts with her forearms. She wanted to put her top back on.

Holding her chin on the top, she quickly stretched her hands from behind to fasten it, but the top fell to the ground again as she lifted her chin. There she was again. Topless on the beach. She had fastened her bra countless times over the years, but this time she knew people were looking and in lifting her chin, she missed. For those around, nothing mattered. People walking and running in the area didn't think for a moment that Melissa's presence was unusual. Only Melissa was self-conscious that she was standing there topless.

Melissa lowered her arms, stood tall, raised her head, and took a deep breath of air. Her chest inflated. She stood erect and proud. Tom didn't stop photographing her in her helplessness and in her rise to individuality. Tom now saw her as a model.

Then, ignoring the shoot, he went over to her, smiled as she lowered her head somewhat, and smiled in return. Within inches away from her, he took his left hand and gently placed it under her chin. Raising her head, Tom stared into her eyes, bent over, and kissed her gently on the cheek. Seconds passed. He paused. He kissed her again moving within an inch of her body, she was frozen, mesmerized.

Tom then led Melissa and the other two girls over to the place where Cecile was sitting for group photographs. Four beautiful girls, one of whom was draped with three strands of pearls. Tom then reached into his equipment bag for another strand of pearls, walked over to Melissa, displayed them in his palms, and proceeded to place the strand around Melissa's neck from behind.

Clasping the pearls, he then moved in front of her and adjusted them on her neck. They were breath-taking. Melissa was hardly breathing. Tom backed off and moved himself beside Fred. Together, they took more and more photos.

Melissa became more comfortable. She looked around and to her surprise, no one was staring at her. She was like every other young woman on the beach. Nothing special, except for Tom.

Cecile, Melissa, and the local girls traded places rotating around Cecile. Their hands folded together on their tummies, by their sides, stretched out in a 'V' formation, over their heads and in other ways, but in all cases, the pearls were the focal point of the shoot.

Ultimately, Tom would make the decision about which photos were to be used in the magazines.

When that part of the shoot was finished. Tom signaled for another break. This time he asked that Cecile and Melissa put their tops back on. The next part would be with cover-ups. But what about the girls? Cecile brought a number of bikinis with her. Fortunately, the tops were large enough, but loose fitting showing much of the young girls' busts. Again, Fred and Tom began clicking away, this time focusing more on the girls and less on the background.

Another 30 minutes flew by. It was now 1 PM. And the shoot was over. Fred packed up the gear, gave Cecile her cheque, and thanked Melanie and Francoise.

"Fred, I'll see you back at the pensione at 4. OK? Melissa and I are going to spend about 30 minutes sunning and swimming before we head back."

"Tom, I will take everything, so you don't have to worry about the equipment and pearls."

"Thanks, Fred."

Tom summoned Melissa to come over. Tom sat down on the towel and then turned over on his back. Melissa did the same as they both closed their eyes and absorbed the heat of the sun. After 10 minutes, Melissa said, "Let's roll over."

She asked Tom to unhook her top so she could get a full tan on her back without strap marks.

"Ten minutes, Tom. No more."

"OK," said Tom.

Tom kept looking at her back, her bum, her legs. Tom was mesmerized.

After about 10 minutes, Melissa piped up.

"I'm hot. Let's cool off in the water."

Melissa rolls over holding her top over her breasts and faces Tom in an upright position. Then, suddenly, she drops her hands, lets her top fall to the ground, and stands up, turns around facing Tom, and says, "Let's go!"

As Melissa runs down to the water, Tom gets up and runs after her. As they enter the water about 3 feet high in the waves, they both dive in head first submerging for a few seconds. And then, after a few strokes out into deeper water over their heads, they come up for air. Swimming within a few metres of each other, Tom can barely touch the bottom. He summons Melissa to come over where she places her hands on his shoulder while treading water.

After a few tense seconds of Melissa holding on to Tom, Tom says, "Time to go! It's getting too hot for me."

"A couple of more minutes. I need to get the sand out of my bottoms."

"Let me help," says Tom.

Melissa giggles as Tom puts his hands on her rear rinsing out the sand.

"OK. I think you got most of it. Let's head back."

They both swim back to shore and walk up to the towels on the sand. Melissa dries herself with the towel, then puts the towel around her waist and removes her bikini bottom, and puts on her shorts. She drops the towel and then puts on a summer top.

With beach bags in their hands, they head back up the cobble stone road to the nearest outdoor cafe.

"Let's stop here. We can get a salad and coffee."

They sit down, order two salads and coffees.

"What happens now with photoshoot? What do you do with all the photographs? There are hundreds."

"Well, I have to review all the photos and start to save the ones for a final review. After hundreds of photos, it really comes down to 20 or 30 that have the 'right' look for a magazine appearance. Here, let's take a look at the camera you used. We can see the photos you took and determine the ones to keep."

Tom hands over Canon camera and puts it in the review mode.

"Here, push the right arrow every time you want to change. If you like a photo, write down the number. The numbers are at the bottom of photo."

Tom's fate was sealed.

Chapter Four
Confrontation

Rick is sitting in his desk chair in his office running through the photographs of the Cap Ferrat trip. No doubt, he was dreaming, now creating a nightmare beyond all proportions.

Staring at blank wall, Rick is clearly somewhere else. Enraged by his father's immoral conduct with Melissa, Rick carefully plans the revengeful act. Almost maniacal and obsessed, sane and insane, focused and unfocused, he plots when, where, and how to do it.

First, he thought of poison in Tom's foods. Oh, too easy, and most likely he would get caught. Then, he thought about changing his medications, but Tom doesn't actively take prescription drugs. Just do it! he thinks. Rage and outrage, his father had and is having an affair with his girlfriend. This is not right. How could he do it? Rick bolts, and wakes up from a cold sweat.

"What a nightmare!" he exclaims. What could he have been thinking? This is heresy. This is the ultimate revenge for his father's lustful conduct.

He turns over photo over photo. Naturally, they're all on the beach. He speeds up, he slows down. His temperature was rising. Sun, sand, and beautiful women. Rick disappears into fantasyland. He missed the trip; the trip was supposed to be with his dad and Melissa. What was he thinking when he turned down the opportunity to go to Cap Ferrat. How could he have let her go with his dad? What's happened to Dad that he had to focus on Melissa? Rick started to analyze the last few years in the household.

Trust, that's it, he thought.

Rick was oblivious to his parent's disintegrating relationship. He didn't think about his mom and dad were growing apart mentally, emotionally, and physically. Rick was so preoccupied himself and in learning the photo advertising business that he missed the signals that his dad was focusing his attention elsewhere and then eventually on Melissa.

Rick looked at the photos more carefully. He pulled out a magnifying glass to examine the images. This was a photoshoot for the International Pearl Association. The pearls had come from farms off the coast of Japan. Cultured, blue with silver reflections; 500 mm in size, and strung together with fine silver thread, enough to make every woman's heartthrob. They were joined with a butterfly clasp embedded with micro-chip diamonds.

Tom had been retained by the International Pearl Association to go to Cap Ferrat and return with sufficient photos for several full-page advertisements for Vanity Fair, Oprah, and Vogue magazines. It was a great contract. One that Tom had been negotiating for the last year.

The International Pearl Association had been a loose association of growers of craftsmen, distributors of jewelry around the world. In 2001, they formed an alliance to control the quality of pearls and to promote their sales. Members of the International Pearl Association met annually at some worldwide convention centres to display their wares. Exhibitors from around the world came to advertise gold, silver, platinum, and other precious metals and stones raw and in jewelry settings.

In Prague in 2004, Tom and Beth attended the conference at the request of the local retailers in Toronto to promote his photography and display ads.

Tom tendered for the contract along with dozens of others. The contract was lucrative and he knew that if he won, his work would be circulated in the major jewelry centres.

Until 2001, Tom had contracts only in North America. He was salivating with his tender. Rick knew this. He knew his father had carefully set out his tender with works that he created over the last several years. This tender meant a lot to Tom. If he got it, the contract would place him in the big leagues of photo advertising.

Looking at the photos, Rick blurts out, "Asshole. What was he thinking?" Rick was now looking at the photos with Melissa in the middle. Dressed in a bikini top and bottom, and then only a bottom. "Dad was intent on making the photoshoot a great success, and I was here, ready to go with him."

"So, what happened? Manny, the general manager, and part owner travelled to Parry Sound for the week to drum up new business for the 'Cottage

Country' magazine. Manny had been in Tom's employ for many years. He knew the business inside and out and was perfect for the new assignment."

Rick was fuming leafing through the photos. He was enraged thinking about his father's conduct. He started pounding the desk.

"Bastard, bastard!" he exclaimed. "He dumped my mother. He fucked my girlfriend."

Rick began mumbling to himself, pacing up and down the floor, smashing the desk, swiping his desk accessories across the floor.

Looking at each photo repulsed him. Tom had taken his own rolls of film with his 35 mm camera as well as his digital camera. Fred, who accompanied Tom and Melissa, took several rolls himself, and the local photographer, on contract, took as many. The photographs from Fred and the local photographer captured almost every twist and turn of the models' movements. The models were so photogenic that selecting a half dozen, and one or two, would be a challenge.

Rick began to slow down, flipping the photos more slowly and looking more carefully. Flipping the photos, staring at them incited him and enraged him. The photoshoot took place on the beach in Cap Ferrat, from 9:30 in the morning to 1 PM. The beaches were empty at the start and filled in by noon. The site on the beach was about 200 feet from the water's edge with the models facing east attracting the morning glow of the sun.

Suddenly, he turned. He went into his father's office where his father kept a selection of handguns. Breaking the glass armoire with a paperweight, he reached for Colt 45, loaded it with six bullets, and ran down the corridor ranting and raving about his father's immoral conduct.

The warehouse film studio was mammoth. Over 30,000 square feet of rooms and more rooms and offices. Photo advertising was a huge business, and Tom had built it up over 20 years from a photo lab in his two-bedroom apartment. Tom's office was at the other end of the warehouse.

Rick found Tom in studio 4. Tom was directing a magazine shoot for cereals. Running down the aisle, yelling at Tom, "You bastard, you bastard. You fucked Melissa. You fucked Melissa."

Rick then raised the gun, pointed it at Tom, and pulled the trigger once, twice, and then a third time. Each time the bullet struck Tom. Tom fell to the floor, blood oozing out of his body. Rick, frozen, dropped the gun. The staff rushed to Tom's side.

Screaming in unison, the staff, reaching for their cell phones, started to call 911 for an ambulance and the police. Others raced over to Rick, tackled him to the ground, and held him down. Rick yielded without so much as a raising a hand in resistance. Staff then pinned him down and used rope to tie his hands and legs until the police came minutes later.

With a 911 call, both two police cruisers and an ambulance arrived several minutes later. While the paramedics helped Tom onto a stretcher, the police handcuffed Rick on the ground, and other officers started questioning the staff.

Rick complied to the nth degree. No resistance, but no talk as well. It appeared that Rick had exhausted all his energy. He turned flaccid. The police had to lift him up and drag out to the car. Tom was off to the Toronto General Hospital, Rick to the 33rd precinct on charges of attempted murder and assault with a deadly weapon.

At the Police Station

Two uniformed police officers lead Rick into an interrogation room, a room 15' x 20' with a simple rectangular table with 4 bridge-like chairs, overhead bright fluorescent lights, and a party wall with a built-in one-way mirror. Nothing else on the walls. They asked Rick to take a seat while they all awaited for a police detective from the murder squad to show up.

Rick was still in a daze. He knew he shot his dad; he knew that the police would be interrogating him and then lay attempted murder charges. He knew that his life was over. He started sobbing. One of the officers stepped out to pick up a tissue box and returned. Meanwhile, two police detectives were peering through the one-way glass mirror watching Rick's conduct. He sat in silence most of the time, sobbing.

Police detectives in the murder squad unit are well-trained in investigating murder scenes and then in questioning persons of interest. They are graduates of the police academy in basic criminal proceedings having taken several courses including vigorous physical exercises in defending themselves and in arresting persons. They take courses in social behavior, criminal law, mediation, psychology, medical assistance, crowd control, and in the use of firearms.

Having passed the basics, police officers may apply for special programs such as the murder squad unit, or the guns and gangs unit. These programs operate for another two years under supervision of training officers who are at the pinnacle of their career or who have since retired or are retiring from the unit and are devoted to impart their skills and knowledge to the younger officers. This continuing education gives the police officer a specialist's degree.

With the two uniformed police officers standing by Rick in the room, Detective Stan Upjohn enters. He is dressed in a two-piece gray suit with a bright light-coloured blue tie. Detective Upjohn in his early 50s having served as uniformed police officer for some 15 years before taking up his specialty, murder and attempted murder cases.

Detective Upjohn was from a family of police officers. His father and his uncle were both police officers before their retirement. He learned some investigating tools from his father who in his later years was assigned as a uniformed police officer to detectives of various units. Detective Upjohn learned to remain cool when examining witnesses and persons of interest in all sorts of criminal activity.

Detective Upjohn then proceeded to upgrade his office by taking the specialist course in murder cases. With family background, Detective Upjohn flew through the course and after two years of part-time training earned a certificate of distinction. He had a great background in resolving murder and murder-like cases.

"Hello, Rick, my name is Detective Upjohn. Can you tell me what happened today?"

Rick remained silent, still sobbing.

"Rick, would you like a cup of coffee?"

Rick did not answer.

"Rick, would you like to use the washroom?"

Rick did not answer.

"Rick, would you like to call a lawyer?"

Rick did not answer.

Detective Upjohn was trying to break the ice. He was getting nowhere. There was no doubt there were witnesses to the shooting. There was no doubt that this was not a case of 'who did it'. This was a case of Rick shooting his father. Were there witnesses? Was it attempted-murder? Did Rick really want to kill his father?

Detective Upjohn then said, "OK, I'll see you later."

Detective Upjohn then left the room and instructed one of the two uniformed police officers to bring in a bottle of water and wait until Rick advised that he had to go to the washroom. Detective Upjohn wanted to hear some words from Rick's mouth before he would officially charge him with attempted-murder or some lesser charge of using a firearm improperly or endangering persons.

Detective Upjohn then proceeded to other examination rooms to speak to eye witnesses who saw what happened. There were several employees who witnessed the shooting. There was a line-up of persons.

After examining just 3 employees, Detective Upjohn knew that he had to make a difficult choice in laying charges. He knew without examining Rick that he could charge Rick with the lesser charge of improperly discharging a firearm or he could charge him with attempted murder. The difference was monumental: serving time for up to 6 months for improperly discharging a firearm or 6 years if convicted of attempted murder.

There was no doubt in Detective Upjohn's mind that Rick would be convicted of either or both charges. However, did Rick have a defence? Surely, he had a defence, thought Detective Upjohn, and that would mitigate the sentence. But would a good defence be sufficient to lower the charges? To excuse him from laying charges at all?

No, a crime had been committed, and he had by training the duty to lay charges. Discretion. That's what he had, discretion.

He had discretion to lay charges on the firing of a firearm or to charge Rick with the attempted murder or both. How was he to exercise that discretion? Was he to flip a coin? Heads, the lower charge; tales, the more serious one. Was he obligated to confer with a more senior detective or even the chief of police? Was he to confer on the Crown Attorney? How was he to decide?

The decision was Detective Upjohn's choice. The senior detective and the chief of police would ultimately say to Detective Upjohn, "You have all the facts; you have sufficient evidence of Rick's wrongdoing; you have his defence; now, it's your decision."

Discretion is defined in case reports as giving the decision maker, and in this case, Detective Upjohn, the right to decide which way to go on resolving an issue.

It was not a simple task. Detective Upjohn should review all those things and more:

- He should confer with a senior detective;
- He should confer with the chief of police;
- He should confer with the Crown Attorney;
- He should confer with Tom to see the depth of animosity;
- He should confer with Rick as to his reasons for shooting his father;
- He should confer with Rick's mom;
- He should conduct a background search on Rick to see if there were other incidents of outrage and violence;
- He should check with Rick's medical reports;
- He should check with Toronto Ace Gun Club as to Rick's disposition.

Ultimately, whatever charges were laid, it's up to the Crown Attorney to recommend the disposition and the Judge to issue the sentence. And even then, Rick or the Crown could always appeal to the Ontario Court of Appeal for a different sentence.

Taking Rick through the judicial system is an expensive journey. The taxpayer has to pay for the police investigations, the use of courthouse and its staff, the Crown attorneys, and the numerous delays in scheduling a preliminary hearing, adjournments and ultimately a trial and possibly an appeal or two along the way to the trial.

On the other hand, Rick has to engage criminal defence counsel. How is he to pick one? How is he able to afford one?

Chapter Five
Meetings with Lawyers

Beth consults her friends. She meets them at the Leslie Golf and Country Club for a lunch. Beth and Tom had been members for years. She had a number of close friends where she played golf as a couple and then with the ladies on Tuesdays. Tom still paid the monthly charges and green fees. But all this was to come to a sudden stop when Tom notified the executive manager to reject any charges made by Beth.

Beth met her friends in the Dining Lounge at 12:30. The 3 ladies were already seated and sipping coffee when Beth arrived.

"How's it going, Beth?" said Denise. "What's happened since last Tuesday? Have you been able to resolve the financial aspects of the separation?"

Beth stared at Denise for several seconds. She did not answer her.

Denise repeated herself. "How's it going, Beth?"

"What's happened since last Tuesday?"

Beth responded. "I'm having a difficult time. Nothing is resolved. We go back and forth with the lawyers with no resolution. It gets heated up. I just want to cry."

"Have you been to Dr. Goldbloom?" said Andrea. "She is usually available. She might be able to give you a referral to a psychologist."

"I don't need a psychologist. I need money. I have no money. I am totally dependent on Tom for everything."

"Look. This is not working out. Thanks, ladies, for your concern and compassion. But I need money."

"I can't stay here for lunch. Thanks for the invitation. But I need help."

Her friends were supportive of the move to stay in the home and file for divorce. This seemed the logical thing to do. But Beth had no money. Beth had no money to pay for the cable and the internet, the telephone, the electricity, the water, the gas. Beth was and is totally dependent on Tom for financial support. How could that have happened?

Beth trusted Tom to take care of her. Beth relied totally on his support. Beth never thought of participating in the running of the home. She expected that she would receive an allowance as did her mother. She didn't know how to participate in the running of the home. Beth never thought about it. Beth recalled that her mother did not participate in the running of the home. Beth's mother was always provided with a weekly salary to pay for the groceries, the laundry, and on occasion, a housekeeper.

Tom wants to meet; Tom wants to explain; Tom wants to reconcile. Bolstered by her friends, and enraged at his conduct, Beth cannot meet face to face.

Could there be reconciliation? How could there be reconciliation when their son shot Tom several times, and now was being charged with possession of a dangerous weapon, discharging a firearm, aggravated assault, and attempted murder. How could Beth reunite with Tom when he was having an affair with Rick's girlfriend and someone almost 14 years his junior? What was Beth to do? Where should she go?

Beth was caught. Beth had few choices. She could attempt to reconcile; she could stick to her instincts and call the marriage over; she could become available and look for someone to take care of her; she could sue for support; she could sue for divorce. All these decisions were before her.

Beth calls and meets with her friends, especially those who were divorced. She wanted to know the names of lawyers who could help. Everyone had a different name! Everyone charged a fortune. But Beth had no money. She called Tom's corporate lawyer, Dave Evans. Dave knew about the shooting, Tom's illness, and the complications that shooting will bring to Tom's company and its possible reorganization.

Beth needed names of lawyers who could help, but who would take on the file without a cash retainer and work on a contingency fee. Dave was concerned that his firm could not act for Beth and Rick even though Dave's firm had two or three family law lawyers. Dave was also concerned that his firm could not act for Rick knowing both Beth and Tom. Dave was conflicted.

Dave recommended that Beth use the internet to find a family law lawyer who would represent her in the negotiation of a support order and terms of divorce. Dave also recommended that Beth contact Legal Aid Ontario which might be of assistance in finding a lawyer to represent her.

Beth started reading 'divorce, separation, custody, legal fees' on the internet. She also read about 'collaborative law' in family law matters. Collaborative lawyers agree not to go to court, but they attempt to resolve the issues by open discussion at the earlier stages of separation. This seemed the right way to go, but Beth would have to make concessions. Her whole life went topsy-turvy overnight.

Beth sat in front of her computer. Looking for the 'right' lawyer was like looking for a needle in a haystack. There were thousands of lawyers in the GTA and trying to find a family law lawyer was a horrendous task. All the websites suggested that their team of lawyers were the best. Many lawyers offered the first interview for free on the internet. Others wanted you to call first to see if you could say enough to get a comfortable feeling about this firm.

Beth decided to shop. She decided to see 3 of them. She made appointments on Monday, Wednesday, and Friday over a two-week period. Beth had done her homework. Conferring with her divorced wives, she compiled one and half pages of questions for the lawyers.

She was ready to visit lawyers.

The first lawyer, Heather Tome, was a woman who was called to the bar less than 5 years ago. She was a sole practitioner having an office in a strip plaza in North Toronto. Beth pulled right up in front of the store. Parked her car, and proceeded to open the door to a small reception where she was greeted by the legal assistant. Beth introduced herself and said that she had an appointment with Ms. Tome. The assistant buzzed Heather on the telephone, and seconds later, Heather came to the front and introduced herself.

Heather led Beth down the hall to a 10-foot by 10-foot meeting room with a rectangular board table and 8 chairs. Heather made Beth welcome. Heather asked Beth to tell her what's going on. Beth was prepared.

"I'm 44 years, married for 24 years. I have two children; Richard, 23 and Wendy, 21. My husband Tom is in advertising. He owns the business which operates out of a warehouse in the lower east side of Toronto. Richard works with him. Wendy is in medical school. She has two years to go before interning. How can you help me?"

Beth asked the questions:

- How long have you been practising family law?
- Do you go to court?
- How often?
- What is your hourly rate?
- Can you give me referrals from clients who were satisfied?
- What are the steps to be taken?
- Do you work on contingency fees?
- What is all this going to cost?
- How long does it take?
- Do you work alone? Or with others?
- Do you have an assistant? Does he or she have an hourly rate? Is he a lawyer?
- ?

Heather asked all her questions, and more.

The meeting went well. Beth was made to feel at home. Heather was soft-spoken and had acted for many distraught women. Heather answered all Beth's questions to Beth's satisfaction. Beth was handed some brochures on family law separations, mediation, and divorce. Heather gave Beth an estimate of legal fees for the divorce at $10,000 as fixed fees and any motions for support at $4,000 for each hearing. All of this plus disbursements and tax.

Beth could not afford this. Beth told Heather that she was broke. No income; no savings; living off the goodwill from friends and gifts from her parents. Heather understood. Heather was prepared to accept contingency fees after the first $5,000 was paid. Beth felt reassured with Heather, but she was concerned about paying her the first $5,000.

Beth asked for references from other clients, but Heather declined as she indicated that her cases and names of clients were confidential except as recorded in the court records. Beth felt comfortable in knowing that her case, that is Beth's case, would remain outside the newspapers. Not that there was anything special about Beth and Tom's marriage and breakup.

Beth didn't want her life story in the newspapers or on local TV. But how could she avoid it? Her son was already front-page news when he was arrested for attempted-murder of his father. Beth was in the spotlight, and there was no way she was going to escape the newsworthiness of her plight against her husband, and the system.

Beth met with the second lawyer, Brad Taylor. He was with a small to mid-size law firm, 10 to 15 lawyers, which covered basic legal work from estates, to collections, corporate, and some family law.

The law firm was on the 35th floor of the Toronto-Dominion Bank tower. For a small to mid-size law firm, it had great presence as you exited the elevator. With glass partitions and windows, you could readily see the Toronto Islands into Lake Ontario. With an open foyer and reception, Beth guessed that the fees would be just too much for her. She was there, and she decided to stay and go through the interview.

Approaching the receptionist, Beth asked for Brad Taylor. The second lawyer, Brad Taylor, had extensive family law background; he wrote family law-related articles for legal newspapers and was a seasonal teacher on divorce and support claims at one of the local community colleges. The receptionist called Brad Taylor and within seconds, he appeared.

Brad was a tall man, dressed immaculately in a two-piece suit and wearing a red patterned tie. He introduced himself, shook Beth's hand, and escorted her to a nearby meeting room, similar in size as the one in Heather Tome's office. They sat down, as he opened his notepad. They proceeded to have a short interview.

As a more experienced lawyer, his fees were based on an hourly rate. He charges $650 an hour. He delegates much of his preparation to his junior associate who charges $250 an hour. He was optimistic about getting a high spousal support order as Tom had a successful business. While Beth liked his approach, she could not afford his rates. After 60 minutes, she thanked him for his time and said she would get back to him as she had to consult her son.

By the time Beth met with the third lawyer, she was in overload. The third lawyer was with a family law firm of women lawyers. Their firm was on Bond Street in a low-rise commercial/office building.

The structure had been renovated with hardwood floors and overhead water pipes, wire crisscrossing the ceiling, and 18" air ducts. The meeting room was more of dining room with a dining room table setup as the boardroom table. It had the feminine touch with flowers, vases, and idyllic paintings, a gas-powered fireplace. Beth met her in the boardroom.

Her name was Jessica Singh. Jessica was friendly, seemed confident, and answered all her questions about what was about to happen. Her fees were in line with those of Heather Tome, and certainly more experienced. Jessica was however prepared to take Beth's case on contingency fees plus $100 an hour if Beth covered all disbursements.

While Beth did not know what those disbursements would be, she asked for an outside amount. Jessica could not pinpoint an amount as the number would change on every motion, assembly of documents, photocopying, court fees, Law Pro litigation levy, and of course the costs of transcripts of examinations. Little did Beth know that such disbursements could cost several thousand dollars.

Beth went home. Confused, frustrated, anxious. Beth diarized her meetings with each lawyer, each one of them. Outside the legal arena, there was no one there to help. Each of the lawyers meant well and could represent her respectably, but she had to go through the whole legal scenario to find out.

Without money, she couldn't get the representation she needed. Could the marriage survive? If not, what was going to happen to Beth? She couldn't talk to Rick, as Rick was on a different planet. His rage against his father clouded his thinking in helping Beth. She was alone.

Years later, Beth realized that none of these lawyers knew what was going to happen. Beth did not know. They did not know. No one lawyer knew what would happen past the initial stages of getting a divorce, getting an order directing spousal support payments, and the ability, or to put more correctly, the inability of collecting the support payments. Her faith in the judicial system went from a high to a low.

From reading other disastrous case reports, she realized that she didn't have a chance in defeating Tom. His lawyers were superb in protecting his rights, and his money. The judicial system was bogged down with red tape, inefficiency in the courts to poor collection and enforcement proceedings.

Beth kept meeting with her single friends. She received free advice. "Be prepared," she kept hearing. She received cocktail advice, settle or fight. That was it.

Mediation vs. litigation. The legal system is designed for civilized people; it is not designed for the rogues of the world who will almost always beat the system for truth and justice. Predictability of the outcome and certainty of the laws, those were the pillars of justice.

This was just another case that no one could predict what would or could happen. Beth needed a lawyer who had a wealth of experience and legal background in troublesome family law break-up, tax law, corporate and estate law, and insolvency background.

Beth subsequently learned the blunt message that once the court imposes an amount to be paid to support creditor, after all appeals, collecting that amount can be an almost impossible task even with the best of lawyers.

Beth was still confused: litigate and bleed, and hope the law is on your side versus mediate through collaborative family law and get what you can based on the assumption that something is better than nothing.

Beth made the easy choice. Off to the courts. Beth wanted revenge. Bleed him. But she had no pocketbook to support that cause. She was hopeless.

Beth didn't know to whom to retain. She had no one to represent her.

Chapter Six
Prosecution

The pistol shots were not life-threatening. They all entered into Tom's left buttock. One bullet grazed his hipbone; the others went into the flesh. Recovery was slow.

Tom spent two weeks in the hospital, most of the time on his stomach. He was irritable and cranky, upset and angry at what had happened and what was happening to the business. He had lots of time to think of Beth, and then Melissa, and then Beth again. He was confused, flustered and unfocused. He called Beth on numerous occasions each day, but Beth did not pick up. For her, the marriage was over.

There would be no chance of reconciliation. She didn't care about the marriage; she didn't care about the children; she didn't care about the laws. She was interested only in protecting herself and getting something, money, out of the marriage of 24 years. What was the tipping point, God only knows. While the marriage had for many years and on many occasions seen good and great times, there were also for many years and on many occasions bad times, abuse, and disinterest.

Melissa on the other hand came to see Tom daily after school. Tom had moved into a spacious condominium in central Toronto. On being released from the hospital, Tom moved into a suite at the Park Hyatt on Bloor Street at Avenue Road so he could be close to Melissa. A little further away, she could still visit Tom at the end of the day and help him get around. Tom needed to change his bandages twice daily and was not able to do this himself. Melissa got first-hand training.

The medical school was just down the street, and so she could walk over after classes and sometimes in between classes. Melissa was in her final year of school. She would graduate and then begin interning.

Melissa was star-struck with awe about Tom. He was so suave, handsome, and tactful. Tom had been gracious, charming, and thoughtful to Melissa while they travelled to Cap Ferrat. She was hooked on love and admiration.

Contrasting with Rick, Melissa knew from within that Tom was the person she could fall in love with and enjoy many years of happiness and adventure. Rick was young, immature, she thought. Rick had a long way to go to win over her love again. His career was just starting, and he lacked foresight as to where his career might take him.

Melissa thought of the many times that they were together, that they would be fighting a lot, and then making up. The emotions between them were either at a high and a low. There was never the constant caring about each other that should have developed over the years.

In the meantime, Beth had packed up his things, all his clothes, his books, his photographic equipment, and anything that could remind Beth of his presence. Away they went to the moving company's storage centre in Mississauga.

Bail Hearing

Rick had been charged with possession of a dangerous weapon, discharging a firearm, assault, and attempted murder. On the following day after the shooting, he was escorted in handcuffs to the Old City Hall where there would be a bail hearing.

In Ontario, once a person is arrested for a crime, the person has the right to be released on bail pending the trial. Bail hearings are usually held before Justices of the Peace to determine whether the accused person is to remain in jail until a trial or whether the accused can be released on terms.

The Old City Hall was built in 1899 to accommodate the growing population of Toronto, then a provincial capital of white Anglo-Saxon origin. For the last 50 years plus, the Old City Hall has been used as criminal court for the Ontario Court of Justice. Up the street and to the west of Old City Hall is the University Avenue Court House for the Superior Court of Justice. The New City Hall is located in the Nathan Philips Square, just west of the Old City Hall.

The Old City Hall building is Romanesque in style, mostly built with sandstone with an imposing clock tower facing south on Bay Street from which at one point of time in the late 19th century one could see the Toronto harbor.

In front of the main entrance is the cenotaph commemorating fallen soldiers from WW I, WW II, and the Korean War during which times Canada sent thousands of soldiers to the other side of the world to defend freedom and democracy. It was a grand old building where the courts meted out justice 5 days a week.

Rick knew nothing about the criminal system in Ontario. He knew no lawyers or even would-be lawyers. There he was before a Justice of the Peace who made inquiries about Rick's charges and his background. Rick was noticeably shaking. What had happened? Reality began to sit in. He shot his father in fit of rage. Was Rick a danger to his father? Was Rick a danger to the public? Those were the questions that had to be answered.

Nicolas Schmidt, of the Crown Attorney's office, had been assigned to the case. Nicolas Schmidt was a seasoned lawyer. He had been called to the Ontario Bar in 1988 and immediately after articling, he joined the Ministry of Attorney General first as a civil litigator and then criminal counsel.

After 10 years of mastering prosecution and appeals, he was appointed senior Crown counsel, criminal division. His specialty was prosecuting members engaged in family violence in the guns and gangs division. Nicolas Schmidt was a force to be reckoned with in the courtroom.

With a police officer on both sides of Rick, the Crown Attorney Schmidt reviewed the circumstances surrounding the charges. He related the scene where Rick ran down to his father's office, yelled at him on several occasions shouting profanities, and then pointed the handgun right at him. Bang, bang, bang, three times before some staff came running across to hold Rick down while others attended to Tom who had collapsed on the floor.

The Justice of the Peace explained to Rick that he had the right to retain a lawyer, or if he could not afford a lawyer, he could apply for legal aid and a lawyer would be provided for him. The Justice of the Peace cautioned him about whether he wished to admit to his guilt or plead not guilty. Rick understood the difference. He, like millions of others, knew the difference between high school and TV soap operas on crimes and criminal law.

But what Rick didn't know was the procedure, the time that all this was to take place, whether he had any defence, and even if he had, whether he should use it, what could happen if he pleaded guilty, and what was going to happen right then and there. Rick had lots of questions, and there was no one there who could answer them for him. He was alone. Beth and Wendy were in the gallery. They sat there sobbing, helpless.

In view of the seriousness of the charges, Crown Attorney Schmidt wanted no bail. He wanted Rick to stay in the detention centre until his trial came up. That could be weeks, no months, and sometimes over a year depending on the volume in the courts at that particular time. Rick said he wanted to find a lawyer. He couldn't go forward today until his lawyer gave him all the answers to his questions.

In less than a minute, Crown Attorney Schmidt argued for continued imprisonment pending the trial. Rick said nothing. The Justice of the Peace set $200,000 as bail. Rick didn't know what that meant. He asked for clarification.

The Justice then proceeded to show Rick a huge orange book. Facetiously, and mumbling to himself, "It's not every day that I hear about a son shooting his own father."

The Justice of Peace thought to himself about what could have gone wrong for a son to shoot his father.

"Here," he said. "There are more than 50,000 lawyers in this province. Pick one. Bail is granted subject to your posting $200,000 with the clerk. Once you post the $200,000, you can be released from jail pending your trial. Officers, please escort Mr. Richardson back to jail."

The hearing was over, in moments. On a murder charge, the Justice of the Peace had to protect the public. He knew that in all likelihood Rick did not have the resources to fund the $200,000 bail order and that if bail should be granted, it should be given at a higher level in the justice system.

Rick was comatose. He was in shock that the Justice of the Peace wouldn't release him. Rick had no money. He was totally dependent on Tom for his salary. He had no money in the bank. He spent every cent on lifestyle, not that he was earning a lot from the business. Whatever he earned, he bought clothes, went out for dinner, spent it on Melissa. There was nothing. Lawyers, he thought, were expensive, how much he didn't know, but he was soon to find out.

He was definitely a candidate for legal aid, unless Beth had money, she could pay a lawyer. But Beth too was on the payroll, and now was cut off. Several months later, his bail application came up again. Rick had enough in the Don Jail, there with all the pimps, drug pushers, and persons charged with sexual assault, murder, and robbery. He realized that he was one of them. The system was against him.

Rick had no job. Rick had no money. Rick could not rely on his mother. Beth had no money too. Beth ran out of money months after Tom vacated the home and cut her off from her bi-weekly pay cheque. Rick turned to Wendy for support, but Wendy now sided with Tom. The family was split down the middle; Beth and Rick were broke, and Tom and Wendy had the money.

Legal Aid Ontario helped Rick. They underwrote Rick's legal defence. They gave him 3 names of criminal defence lawyers who had some experience in defending persons who were charged with serious crimes. However, the choice was up to Rick as to whom he chose.

Rick had to get out of jail. But he had no money for bail. He had already been in jail for over 4 months with no end in sight as to when his case might be heard. Rick stalled on calling any of these 3 lawyers hoping that his mother might come up with the bail money. Wishful thinking on his part. Beth had her own problems coping with a failed marriage, a son who took the law into his own hands, and a daughter who sided with the father.

The Toronto South Detention Centre provided private rooms for interviews with lawyers. They also provided telephones so persons could contact lawyers for assistance and representation. Rick had the coordinates of all 3 lawyers in his hand. "Which one should I choose? What should I tell them? How will I know that he/she is best for me?"

Rick calls lawyer A. "Hello, my name is Rick Richardson. I have been charged with attempted murder of my father."

Rick had a series of questions for the lawyer.

"Do you take legal aid?

"Do you charge more than legal aid?

"Can you tell me if you have represented persons accused of murder before? How many?

"Can you represent me?"

Lawyer A paused. "Are you the guy that shot his father several months ago? I read about this in the newspapers."

"Yea, that's me."

"Where are you?"

"I'm in the Toronto South Detention Centre. I don't have any money to pay the bail."

“How much is it?”

“$200,000.”

“Did Legal Aid give you a number?”

“Yeah, 19-4689.”

“OK.”

“I can come and see you on Wednesday after 2. We can talk about it then.”

“No, I want to know if you have defended others who have been charged with attempted murder. Can you tell me?”

“I had one case 3 or 4 years ago.”

“What happened?”

“He was convicted.”

Click. Without asking questions about the trial, Rick hung up. Rick was tense. That lawyer was not for him.

Rick called lawyer B. Rick was more confident in asking questions.

“Hello, my name is Rick Richardson. I have been charged with attempted murder. I am presently in the Toronto South Detention Centre and I cannot afford bail. Is there any way to get of here without posting the $200,000 bond that the court ordered me to pay?”

“Thank you for calling. My name is Jack Reiter. I think you want to speak to my brother, Morris Reiter. He practices criminal law. Can you hold for a minute and I will get him?”

“Hello, this is Morris Reiter. Are you looking for a defence lawyer?”

“Yes, but I have got to get out of jail first.”

“What’s your legal aid number?”

“19-4689.” No sooner than Rick gave his number, Morris told him that he would come over to the Toronto South Detention Centre tomorrow morning after 10, and then Morris hung up the phone.

Momentarily, Rick was pleased. Then, he thought that he never put the questions to Mr. Reiter and he really didn’t know anything about him.

✱✱✱✱✱✱✱✱✱✱✱✱✱✱✱✱

Morris Reiter attends the Toronto South Detention Centre. Immediately following the call with Rick, he called the Toronto South Detention Centre, booked a meeting room, and found out the name of the Crown counsel who was handling the case. Morris called the Crown’s counsel and requested a copy of the Crown's report. It was sent over hours later in an email for Morris to read before the appointment.

Clearing security, Morris meets Rick in a meeting room. They shake hands and sit down at a table across from each other.

Rick: "You've got to help me. I'm in this place with crooks, gangsters, pimps, and murderers. You've got to get me out of here."

Morris: "Hello, Rick. I'm Morris Reiter. You called me yesterday, and here I am today ready to help. I've read the police report and the Crown Attorney's report on the bail hearing. You're here because you shot your father with a gun. Right. You didn't kill him. You shot him only in the butt. That's attempted murder in anybody's books."

"I was only trying to scare him, not kill him. As much as I hate him now for what he's done to my mom, I didn't have any intention to kill him."

"Tell that to the judge. It's a tough one to swallow," said Morris.

"But we're not there yet, first we have got to get you out of here."

"The bail is set at $200,000. You obviously don't know how that amount was set. I suppose you can't get that kind of money from your mother. Is there anyone else that can help you?"

"There's my sister. But she doesn't have any money, and besides, she sides with my father."

"Have you ever been charged before?" says Morris.

"No," replied Rick.

"Have you ever committed a driving offence? Such as speeding? Or leaving the scene of an accident?"

"No," replied Rick.

"Are you still living at home with your mother?"

"Yes."

"Have you a passport?"

"Yes."

"Have you spoken to your father since the shooting?"

"No."

Morris pauses. Should he or shouldn't he ask the question "Why did you shoot him?"

Morris knew the answer to the question without so much as Rick responding. But he thought he better hear the explanation for himself.

"Tell me what happened."

"Do you mean, why did I shoot my father?"

"OK, tell me what happened."

Rick sighs. He takes a deep breathe. "I was upset. I was angry. He took my girlfriend to Cap Ferrat on an advertising assignment to take photos of women wearing fancy pearls. He took advantage of her. He had her on the beach topless and wearing a brief bikini bottom. She even showed up in part of the photoshoot.

"Damn him. I saw the photos on his desk back here in Toronto. I was so enraged that I took his gun that he kept behind his desk in the credenza. I knew it was there after we had a robbery several years ago. He bought a gun and used to give it to me when I took up target shooting at the Toronto Ace Gun Club on College Street."

"How long have you been target shooting?"

"About six years."

"How good are you?"

"I am considered a 'sharpshooter'. I won the yearly trophy for marksmen for the last 5 years."

"What does that mean?"

"Well, I can shoot an apple sitting on a pedestal 50 feet away."

"Out of 10 shots, how many times would you hit it?"

"Ten times," said Rick.

Rick grew up with guns. Tom had started a collection when he was a young teenager. Tom had over 50 hand-guns that were manufactured around the world. As a teenager and throughout Tom's university, Tom participated in gun clubs. Tom was a proficient marksman.

When Rick was barely 5 years old, Tom would take him to the range for practice. Rick had a flashback to when he was a kid. He recalled that he soon became a marksman in his own right.

At 15, he entered the contest at the Toronto Ace Gun Club for the marksman of the year under 16. There was no competition. Rick won the trophy easily defeating the nearest rival by a landslide. He started winning gun matches. After his first major trophy, he went on to win many more. But he respected guns. He knew they were not toys, but dangerous instruments.

Morris interjects, "Why do you think he had a relationship with her?"

"When they returned to Toronto, she was rather cold to me and kept on telling me what a fabulous time she had with him."

"But do you know if he seduced her?"

"I know he did. He did. I know it."

"Did she tell you?"

"No."

"Did your father tell you?"

"So, how do you know?"

"Well, I guess I don't know—But my gut tells me he did."

"Let's see if we can get you out of here. Sometimes in cases where you're not a danger to the public, the judge might let you out pending the trial on the condition that you do not leave your home. Do you think that you could live with that?"

"Sure, no problem."

"Rick, you could be at home for over one year before the trial takes place. That's a very long time to remain in your home."

Morris told him that his trial must occur within 18 months of the charges. His rights under the Charter dictated that special right.[1]

"Can I go outside into the backyard?"

"Likely. You also have to wear a leg band that monitors your whereabouts. If you wander outside your home onto the street, you would be in breach of your bail. In that case, you can expect that the police will pick you up and transport you back to the Don Jail or the Toronto South Detention Centre."

"Can you live with that?"

Rick nods his head up and down.

Morris was an experienced criminal defence lawyer. He had been practising for over 25 years. He knew most of the Crown attorneys, and particularly Crown Attorney Schmidt.

After a couple of telephone conversations with Nicolas Schmidt, Morris then makes the arrangements with the Crown Attorney and attends before another Justice of the Peace to vary the initial order to provide Rick's release on the express condition that he remain in the family home and wear an ankle

---

[1] *Re Askov* 1990 SCC 45. Under s. 11(b) of the *Charter of Rights*, any person charged with an offence has the right to be tried within a reasonable time. The primary aim is to protect the individual's rights and to protect fundamental justice for the accused and for the community to see justice is done in a timely manner. The effect of delaying justice may cause memories to fade over time, and witnesses who may move away, become ill or die.

bracelet until the trial failing which he will be returned to jail. On the day of the trial, he will attend with his lawyer from the home to the courthouse.

The Trial

On a cold wet November day, one year and two months after the shooting, Beth and Wendy headed down to the Old City Hall for Rick's trial. The rain was beating down on Beth's car to such an extent that she was driving 30 km an hour following the Bay Street bus south to the waterfront. On reaching Queen Street, Beth turns right, along Queen Street driving into the parking lot under New City Hall.

Driving down the ramp you could see little balls of perspiration, the sweat on her face, dealing with the pressure of the trial and anticipating her son's trial and the foul weather. Relieved momentarily, she passes under the cover of the pedestrian square above. She reaches for a ticket, passes it to Wendy, and proceeds down 3 ramps to find the first available parking space.

The two women had been silent for the last half hour since they left their home. Their anticipation as to what was going to happen had been going on for several months. Their anxiety levels were high as were their nerve endings.

On exiting the car, Beth falls to the cement ground. She caught her heel of her right foot on the ledge of the door, and down she went. She scrapped her right knee. Wendy runs around the car and positions herself as a crutch as she helps her mother rise. Barely breaking the skin, Wendy whips out some facial tissues and dabs her mother's knee now bleeding down her leg.

"OK, I'm all right," says Beth, her voice quivering with nerves and pain. "Let's go or we'll be late. We can't miss this one."

Leaving the city hall parking, they walk arm-in-arm and open their huge golf umbrellas to a steady downstream of rain that was blowing against them. Not adequately dressed for the foul weather, the rain immediately soaked their shoes, their feet, and the lower part of their legs as their raincoats were three-quarter lengths.

They were walking only a few hundred metres away to the front door of the Old City Hall at Queen Street entrance. On climbing up the stairs, they closed their umbrellas so they could enter the doors, and they shook the water off their coats. Their faces were wet with rainwater, sweat, and tears as they looked around this old cavernous building that housed many of Toronto's criminal trials.

The information desk at the front hall had all the postings of the day including the name of the accused, the courtroom, and the presiding judge. The list was spread out over twenty pages of named accused, alphabetically.

The commissioner, a man in his mid-70s, gray and white hair with black rim eyeglasses, wearing a dark blue suit, a matching colour peaked hat with an official commissioner's badge depicting Ontario Justice symbols on the breast pocket of his jacket, was on the other side of the desk inquired from the women where they were going. In a courteous and official manner, the commissioner said.

"The case is being heard by Judge Carnworthy in courtroom 103. What's he like?" said Wendy.

"Oh, he's tough on crime, but ends up giving most of them a decent punishment."

"What's that mean?" interjects Beth.

"For the simple crimes, stealing from a bookstore, defrauding on your credit card, he gives you a lecture, but then if the guy apologizes, he gives him an easy sentence. You know, 6 months in jail and 6 months cleaning the streets. The parole board automatically reduces a third of the sentence."

"My God. What did Ricky do? The judge will never understand that he didn't mean it."

On thanking him, Beth and Wendy headed down the left corridor to courtroom 103. Seconds later, they attempted to open the door. The courtroom was packed. Standing room only. Dozens of people in all sorts of garb, dozens of people of different colours and speaking different languages, and little kids running around and around.

No doubt Beth and Wendy were overdressed for the occasion. Friends and family of the accused were commiserating with one another. There was no place to sit. There was no place to stand. They couldn't get in. Beth started to sob, tears running down her cheeks, her nose all clogged up. She couldn't enter the courtroom to see her son.

"Wait her, Mom. Don't move from the entrance. I'm going back to the front desk to see if the commissioner can help us."

Wendy then scooted down the hall and accosted the commissioner. "Help me, please. I can't get into the courtroom where my brother is."

"What's he charged with?" said the commissioner.

"Why is that important?"

"Well, if it is serious, there will be extra police around and they'll screen everyone for guns and knives."

"What? Can you help me?"

The commissioner, obviously a senior citizen who probably worked in the government, was earning a bit more by being a goodwill ambassador had shown some concern over Wendy's plight. The commissioner got on the phone and called his buddy, Max, in courtroom 103.

"Hey, Max," yelled Jack. "I've got two ladies in distress. They want to get into Judge Carnworthy's court, but the place is jammed. I think this one is the sister of what's his name?" addressing Wendy.

"Ricky. I mean Richard Richardson."

"What's he charged with?"

"Attempted murder and other charges."

"Max, can you get them in? Yes, no, yes."

Jack then leaned over the desk. "Miss, Max will come out to get you. Don't worry. He's a good guy, but your brother is in one hell of a mess. Good luck."

Wendy hustled back to courtroom 103. Max opened the door from the inside.

"Move away, move away," Max exclaimed in front of a large number of people who were "hanging around" the door to the court. Max had learned to control groups of people who often congregated in and about the courtroom.

Showing some officialness, Max yelled, "Here, here, in the name of the Queen all persons having dealings in courtroom 103, please enter now. All persons who have no business in courtroom 103, please leave immediately."

With those words, people began trading places. The session was about to begin. Police officers moved to the front of the door. Two officers remained inside the courtroom at the entrance.

"Ma'am, miss, come over here. I will escort both of you and find some places to sit. Come on, the judge is about to come in."

Beth and Wendy entered the courtroom with escort. Max took them right up front to an empty row usually reserved for senior counsel. Not today. No senior counsel had signed in. So, Beth and Wendy had an almost front row view of the judge.

Max, addressing the courtroom, "To those who remain in the courtroom, please turn off your cell phones. If your cell phone rings while the court is in session, the judge will order you to deliver up your cell phone to the court clerk who will impound your cell phone until you pay a fine of $200. So, turn off your cell phones."

"Here, here, everyone stand," Max yelled. The judge entered from the rear door on the left side of the dais and promptly sat down. Max then yelled, "Anyone having dealings with Her Majesty, the Queen, in this courtroom, please sign in. The Honourable Justice Cantor presiding."

Justice Cantor was substituting for Justice Carnworthy who was transferred that morning to a different courtroom. Justice Cantor was known for his 'no nonsense' approach and on conviction usually followed the Crown Attorney Counsel's recommendation as to prison sentence.

The judge reviewed his docket sheet, seven matters on for today. Most of them were held over for sentencing. Two of them were slated for summary trials, although one of the persons on the list indicated that he was going to plead guilty and wanted to get the matter over with. Rick Richardson was the third matter.

Max signaled the police officers to bring in number 1, Abraham Rajab. This was a hearing for sentencing. Abraham Rajab was a young man charged and convicted several weeks ago for dangerous driving while under the influence of alcohol. This was his third time up for similar offenses.

The Crown Attorney read a brief summary of the case. Abraham Rajab was speeding his 2013 Porsche on Highway 400 going 155 km on the evening of August 13, 2014. He was caught racing back and forth from the inside lane to the outside lane for at least 3 kilometres thinking that he was at the Exhibition on the kiddy car track. His blood alcohol reading was in excess of 1.5 mg.

While Police Office Carry did not impound his car, he drove it to the nearest rest area for pick up. His colleague, Police Officer Brown, escorted Abraham Rajab to the Finch/Dufferin detention centre for the night. The Crown recommended that he be imprisoned for 2 months, be required to attend 16 community high schools for 16 hours to speak about the damages that drinking and driving causes and that his licence be canceled for 5 years.

Mr. Rajab was not represented by counsel. Instead, his father appeared and pleaded that he not be sent to jail. After pausing for a short second, the judge said, "No, I am sorry, Mr. Rajab Sr. Your son has not learned a valuable lesson. He is fortunate that he did not injure anyone or cause property damage. In either case, he would have been sent to jail for 2 years without any chance to be released at an earlier time.

"Mr. Rajab Jr., consider yourself fortunate. You are sentenced to 3 months imprisonment and you are required to attend 20 high schools within one year following your release for 20 one-hour sessions on why you were speeding and drinking alcohol. Your driver's licence is canceled for 5 years."

Max signaled another set of officers to bring up No. 2. Ephraim Carlye. The Crown read a brief summary of the case. Ephraim Carlye was caught shoplifting in the Hudson Bay Department Store on Queen Street West in Toronto on May 10. Mr. Carlye had used his backpack to camouflage his lifting precious jewels having a value of over $30,000.

Mr. Carlye would place his backpack on the jewelry counter and then open up a compartment on the bottom. While the clerk was fetching a jewelry piece from the other side, Mr. Carlye had access to a tray of other jewels. Were it not for the closed-circuit television, he would have escaped with the jewels undetected. The Crown Attorney recommended 3 years imprisonment.

"Abbass M., for Ephraim Carlye, Your Honour. Mr. Carlye is 34 years old. He lives with his ailing mother. He works for Whirlpool Washing Machines on an assembly line inserting parts. He makes minimum wages. He has never been in trouble before. I submit that he should perform community service rather than be imprisoned."

"Anything else, Mr. Abbass?"

"No, Your Honour."

"Mr. Carlye, do you have anything to say before this Court sentences you on your conviction."

"No. I hired Mr. Abbass to defend me. I am counting on him to help."

"Mr. Carlye, please stand. It is the judgment of this Court that you be imprisoned for 3 years. Officers, please escort Mr. Carlye out of the court."

Pause.

Max signaled another set of officers to bring up No. 3. Richard Richardson. Justice Cantor then says to Mr. Richardson.

"Where is your lawyer?"

Richard replies, "I think he is in the washroom."

Crown Attorney Nichola Schmidt rises. "Sir, can we put this down for 15 minutes?"

"No problem, Mr. Schmidt."

Mr. Schmidt leaves to find Morris Reiter. When he sees him in the hallway, Mr. Schmidt approaches him and advises that they were called and that the judge gave a short adjournment.

"Mr. Schmidt, can we agree on the facts or do you want us to call witnesses?"

Mr. Reiter was concerned about calling Rick to the stand and explain the circumstances surrounding the shooting.

Morris told him that it is not common for the accused to take the stand. In fact, in most criminal cases, defence counsel never calls the accused to testify. He told Rick that the Crown Attorney must show 'beyond a reasonable doubt' that Rick intended to murder his own father. Because of the unique circumstances, Morris recommended that Rick give up his right to have a jury and that he be tried before a judge alone.

"Yes," Rick said.

Not knowing any better, he relied on Morris. So, there it was. The Crown Attorney was to read into the record the facts surrounding the case. Morris recommended that Rick plead not guilty to a charge of attempted murder, but plead guilty to the charge of discharging a firearm.

He thought calling the mother, father, and sister, and that he could turn the judge around into believing that this case was not about protecting the public so much but protecting the family unit. There was obviously a need for family law crisis centres. Rick agreed.

Crown Attorney Nicholas Schmidt states the facts, "Namely, on 13 October, Richard Richardson ran down the hallway at the warehouse on 2350 Lauder Avenue and there, armed with a 45 handgun shot Thomas Richardson, his father, 3 times in the right lower back buttock. Richard Richardson clearly admits that he shot his father, but denies any intention to kill his father. In fact, Richard Richardson is considered to be an excellent marksman, and that if he wanted to kill his father, he would have done so."

"Well, Mr. Reiter. Do you agree with these facts?"

"Yes, Your Honour."

Justice Cantor looking at Rick and says to him, "Well, Mr. Richardson, in view of these facts, How do you plead to the charge of attempted murder. Guilty or not guilty?"

"Not guilty, Sir."

"How do you plead to the charge of discharging a firearm?"

"Guilty, Your Honour."

"OK, Mr. Schmidt, do you have any witnesses to call?"

Crown Attorney Nicolas Schmidt replies, "Your Honour, in light of the agreed facts, the Crown has no witnesses."

"Mr. Reiter," the judge says, "How does the defence wish to proceed?"

"We wish to proceed without a jury and before a judge alone. My client will be testifying. I also intend to call his mother and his father."

On hearing this, the judge says to both counsel, "We are going to have a short recess for about 25 minutes. Please gather your notes and wait for the Registrar who will escort you to the Judge's Chambers."

The Judge rises. The Registrar shouts, "All rise, this court is adjourned to 11:45. Please remain standing until the Judge leaves the courtroom."

Judge's Chambers

The Registrar leads Mr. Schmidt and Mr. Reiter through the back door of the court down a narrow hallway to a meeting room. Mr. Schmidt and Mr. Reiter have known each other for many years.

"What do you think the judge is doing?" says Morris. "He's done this once before a few years ago when he realized that he might be biased. But this time, I haven't a clue."

"I don't think that's the case here," says Nick. "I think he's contemplating some sort of family therapy."

"What do you mean?"

"Well, from the agreed facts, there's no doubt he shot his father in rage. That's a criminal offense and a serious one at that. On the other hand, in the circumstances of the case, his mother's separation, his sister's siding with the father, and the father having a relationship with the accused's girlfriend, we have a family law crisis."

"I think that the judge really doesn't want to try this case."

The Registrar then escorts the lawyers into the Judge's Chambers.

"Gentlemen, please take a seat."

"Where are we going with this case, Nick?"

Nick pauses. Morris speaks up. "It's pretty cut and dried," says Morris. "He shot his father out of rage. He is a marksman. He is an excellent shooter. If he wanted to kill his father, he would have done so. The difficulty I see is the nature of the punishment. This is a family law crisis that needs to be addressed. Unfortunately, our judicial system is not set up for this. He's no danger to the public, only his father. Any other case, he would get 3 to 6 years in imprisonment, and with parole, he would be out in a year."

"Nick, what do you think?"

"Well, Your Honour, I agree with Mr. Reiter. Rick was working with his father in the advertising business. I don't think that's possible anymore. He has to go back to school to learn a trade. In view of the family breakup, I suggest that he be placed under house arrest for nine months after which time he must attend a community college of his choice for a new career."

"Nick, do you agree?"

"Yes."

"Well, that's it. Consider it done."

Chapter Seven
Preparing for the Fight

Retaining Lawyers

Beth chooses her lawyer. Tom chooses his lawyer.

What did Beth know about lawyers? Nothing. She went to high school and University in Toronto, and on obtaining her Bachelor of Science and her M.R.S. in the same year, some of her classmates went on to medical school and law school. These friends were business people, and with some professionals.

Beth was alone. What did she know about her situation? Public school didn't teach her about how to be a good daughter, how to be a good wife, and how to be a good mother. She learned the hard way, making many mistakes along the way, still making mistakes, and was still learning. She now had to find a lawyer to fight her husband. Not just any lawyer, but one who would represent her well. Shopping for lawyers was not so easy. It was far easier to shop for a pair of shoes than to find the 'right' lawyer.

Her parents, while still alive, rarely dealt with lawyers in their lifetime. They had no contact with lawyers. A will for each of them, a lawyer acting on purchasing their home, then another lawyer when they purchased their condominium, that was the extent of what her parents knew about lawyers.

Beth called her friend, Joyce Crothers. "Help, I need help."

Family law issues in Ontario are an imploded hornet's nest. Domestic violence was on the rise. Almost everyone gets stung sooner or later. Family law issues involve not only custody issues over who gets access to the children, when, how long, and where, but also the size and duration of support payments. Litigation is stressful; no one can predict the outcome; very few can afford the costs. Litigation is a 'lose, lose' situation in almost every situation.

Emotions run high and often cloud the judgment of the parties involved out of the need for spite or revenge. Is someone in immediate danger? Is it possible that Tom would strike Beth? Did Beth fear for her well-being, her life? Did Beth fear that Tom would strike her? Beth didn't have those fears.

Instead, she feared his verbal abuse to the point where they could not talk to each other. Was Beth to leave home or go to a shelter? How could she keep the home? She had no income to pay for the mortgages, the utilities, let alone money for food. Forget clothing, manicures, and hair salons. There was no surplus income for these luxuries.

Beth was no different from the thousands of women who were abandoned by their husbands and mates for newer relationships. Did Beth have to leave the matrimonial home? Did she need shelter away from Tom?

Beth confided in Joyce. They met at Macy's Premier Coffee House on Bloor Street West on the morning of May 11. Beth was first embarrassed to tell her parents that her marriage was failing, and past the point of no-return. The marriage had broken down, and it was beyond repair. As often said, there were irreconcilable differences between Beth and Tom.

Joyce listened and listened. And then after the second round of coffee, Joyce perked up and said to Beth, "Let's sleep on this for a few days. There are lawyers at Jones, Wilson, and Company that deal with this. I don't know any of them directly, but I do know Arnold Jones and trust his judgment. Let's see."

"Who are Jones Wilson?" Beth replied. "I don't need a real estate lawyer. I need a family law lawyer who can rip Tom apart and get me a good settlement."

Arnold Jones had gone to school with Joyce. He was at an established law firm in Toronto. Although he had some background in litigation, he did not practice family law.

"Give me some time," said Joyce. "Let me get back to you on Monday."

Monday came and passed. Beth became overly anxious. She thought Joyce would get back to her quickly. Instead, Beth called her, and on answering the call, Joyce said she had spoken to Arnold Jones, and he was debating about using 2 lawyers in his firm.

With a new client, Arnold was not about to recommend Beth to another law firm, even if he thought that the other law firm was better equipped. No, Arnold had to choose between lawyers in HIS firm, to keep his lawyers busy.

Joyce trusted Arnold but suspected that Arnold's delay and his recommendation may not be good enough for Joyce's long-standing friend.

Arnold debated between Kevin Alexander and Heidi Matthews. Kevin had more experience but he was more expensive. But Arnold thought a woman may be more effective in dealing with the situation. Arnold thought that Tom would be intimidated by a woman lawyer.

Heidi, despite her good nature personality, she was no withering flower. She could hold her own against most lawyers. And so, ultimately, Arnold recommended Heidi and told Joyce to make the arrangements for a meeting between the two. Heidi was a solid lawyer; she knew her stuff. She knew how to prepare materials on both sides.

However, she lacked the assertiveness of a combatant litigator. Not that she needed to be a forceful litigator. In most cases, the material if prepared well, speaks for itself before a judge. Heidi was well-suited for the assignment.

Beth was relieved. She had never shopped for a lawyer and didn't have the know-how to get one who could really help. Joyce set up the meeting.

Beth fretted over the week. The last time she met with a lawyer was when she and Tom bought the house, many years ago. And that was on a happy occasion. This meeting was to be a somber meeting with a woman she had no connection with. Beth was intimated. She didn't know what to expect; she didn't know what to do in preparation; she didn't know what questions to ask; she didn't know anything about her. Beth had no one to call for assistance in dealing with lawyers.

On May 26, Beth went to see Heidi at her office at 151 Yonge Street. They met in one of the meeting rooms. Heidi together with an articling student took down all the introductory information about Beth and then proceeded to ask questions about the marriage breakdown.

After 2 hours of intense questions and answers, Beth was wiped. Heidi, on the other hand, had begun to focus on the family law issues and Beth's need for financial and emotional support. The children, being over 18, no longer required child support although both children wanted to pursue higher education.

Heidi had conducted interviews over and over. She was no stranger to family breakups. Heidi conveyed emotional stability to Beth who was reluctant to answer many personal questions about their marriage. After two hours of intense examination, Heidi concluded the first meeting with a boost of enthusiasm for Beth's case. Heidi suggested another meeting or two so that she could get the full story and begin by drafting the divorce papers and materials for a preliminary attack on Tom.

"We need to get a support order first. That means we set up a hearing in the family court for an order that Tom pays you once a month. We'll talk about the amount later. Let's meet next week," said Heidi. "I need to get your income tax returns for the last 5 years. Can you get me Tom's as well?"

Beth was totally dependent on Tom since the day of their marriage. Beth knew very little about the business structure or the financing. What she did know was whether the business was doing well. Tom always told her the business temperature on a regular basis.

At first, the business struggled; and then with more advertising, the business picked up over several years. Beth was primarily focused on her $1,000 weekly salary so she could shop for food, buy clothes for herself and for the children and pay for the housekeeper. All other expenses were paid by Tom. While Beth was aware of the expenses, she did not know the numbers. And while the relationship matured, she had no reason to question anything except asking now and then for a raise.

Beth told Heidi that she would have difficulty in getting all those tax returns. They were on Tom's personal computer. When Tom left, he took his computer with him.

"Are there hard copies of your returns anywhere?" asked Heidi.

"I'll check," said Beth, "but I doubt it."

"What about the accountant? Who did Tom use for himself and the business?"

"Aaron Rothberg. He is an old friend of Tom's. He has his office with A & L, a national accounting firm in downtown Toronto."

"Can you call him up?" said Heidi. "He should be able to send you copies of your returns. Ask him to send copies of Tom's and the business?"

"Do you think that he would do that?" replied Beth. "I'm sure Tom has already spoken to him about our marriage breakup. Do you think that I have a chance?"

"There's nothing to lose," said Heidi. "In the worst-case scenario, we can get them with a court order."

"OK, I'll try."

As expected, Beth was only able to get her own tax returns. Aaron told her that he has spoken to Tom and that he, Tom, refused to give his consent. Aaron was divided between the two. But, leaned in favour of Tom as his friend, and in preserving the business account, he was not disclosing the other tax returns. That was enough for Heidi to prepare a preliminary motion for support.

Heidi knew her law. She knew with information from Beth she could put together motion material for an order of support. Beth's tax returns showed that Tom had put her on salary at $9,000 a month for the last few years, that he had a RRSP account with $250,000 plus in forced savings.

Round One. The Court Day—1st of Many

September 15. That's the day that Beth scores a minor TKO. The court orders Tom to pay $5,000 monthly until further order of the court or to the conclusion of the divorce proceedings. That was the end result after 13 attendances before the family court over a year and one half.

The first attendance was back in February. Heidi set up the date and coordinated it with the court staff and with Arthur Gopple, Tom's lawyer. Heidi had served her motion record with Beth's affidavit requesting an interim order of $9,000 monthly until the divorce hearing.

Heidi met with Beth at the entrance of 393 University. Beth was with her son Rick and her mother, Mrs. Avery. They went up the elevator and got off on the 9th floor, cleared security, and then appeared in front of courtroom 906. The daily list was posted on the marquis. They were number 18. Heidi was already gowned and carried a large satchel of documents and case law.

"Let's go into the courtroom and get settled. I have to check in with the clerk and wait our turn on the docket list. We are number 18 on the list of 35. Not so bad," says Heidi.

"We are going to be on the right side. So, Beth, please sit here. Rick and Mrs. Avery, please sit beside Beth."

Usually, there is a long list of matters to be dealt with, many never go on and others are settled before the court convenes.

It's 9:50. And the court starts to fill up with families. Then Arthur Gopple appears, also gowned, along with Tom and their daughter Wendy. Arthur points to seating on the left side of the court suggesting that they get some seats before they are all gone.

At 10:00, the Registrar announces that all parties having cell phones turn them off before the judge arrives and requests everyone stand up as the judge enters the courtroom.

At 10:00, there is not a seat to be had. Many are standing at the rear of the court, still with their coats on. On the two aisles leading up to the dais are several little children on the floor with coloured pencil crayons and paper with their mommies, and daddies, peering over to watch their safety.

The Judge says, "Good morning, everyone, boys and girls, let's get started. Registrar, are there any matters that are being adjourned?"

The Registrar notes two and requests that the lawyers for the first one stand up and speak to the adjournment. Both lawyers agree that they need time to prepare and that they will need at least ½ day to argue the case. The judge says, "Well, that cannot be today. You will have to book this with the court office."

As the lawyers for the second adjournment rise, the courtroom hears two kids crying in the aisle.

"Whose children are these?" says the judge. Seven people get up. Mothers, fathers, grandmothers, and grandfathers rise.

"Do these children not know what a court is?" asked the Judge. Then seven people started talking, one over-talking the others.

"Hold it, everyone, we need some decorum here. Please pick up your child or grandchild and tell them where they are." That lasted for about 10 minutes when the children went back to the aisles to play with their crayons and paper.

"Are there any contested adjournments?" said the Registrar.

Five or 6 lawyers stand up. "Let's deal with the first contested adjournment on the daily list."

One lawyer says that his client was served 2 days ago and needs time to respond.

Another lawyer says her opposing lawyer is stuck in traffic on the 400 south of highway 89 and will not be able to attend until after 3 this afternoon.

A third lawyer says that he wants time to prepare and file a responding affidavit.

A fourth lawyer stands up and indicates that he wants to cross-examine the other spouse.

A fifth lawyer stands up and says that he wants to remove himself from the record.

After 2 hours of dealing with adjournments, consent matters, and contested adjournments, the Judge finally says, "Now, we can deal with the remaining matters after lunch. Instead of taking a morning break, I think we should adjourn until 2 PM when we will deal with the remaining cases."

"All rise."

And so, it was for Beth and Heidi. One adjournment after another; some on consent, others contested for one reason or another. Seven different judges over a period of 18 months. No one judge took carriage of the case. There were just too many cases lined up for hearings.

The second hearing through to the 12th hearing were pretty well the same. Crowded courtrooms, kids all over the room, babies crying, one family on the left and the other family on the right, requests for adjournments, debates about adjournments and then consent matters, real consent matters, and not just those thinking the matter was on consent. The Judge and court staff were wiped out by 1 PM. Everyone needed a break.

In response to Beth's affidavit, Arthur and Tom discussed whether to cross-examine Beth on her affidavit. Tom had a right to file an affidavit in reply, but they chose not to do so as he would have to disclose some of his assets.

The cross-examination was set up. Heidi and Beth could not understand why Tom wanted a cross-examination. Everything in her affidavit made sense and was right. It appeared that the examination was a stalling tactic since they had to keep adjourning the motion for a support order. First, there had to be the setup; then the examination that lasted more than one day; then the transcript. Several months passed before they were back on track with the motion for support.

Over the summer, Heidi prepared a motion record for an interim order requiring Tom to pay Beth $9,000 a month. Heidi prepared a lengthy affidavit in Beth's name setting out the circumstances of the separation, the divorce proceedings, and sufficient material to show that despite the separation, Beth was entitled to receive $9,000 monthly based on her income for the last several years from Tom's company.

Under the threat of an interim motion for delivery of Tom's tax returns, Tom's new counsel conceded. Tom's new counsel was Tim Harrigan, a civil litigator with a boutique law firm in downtown Toronto. Tom initially approached his company lawyers, also known for their separate litigation arm,

Abrams, Baker & Censori, Litigators (ABC Litigators) for a civil litigator in family matters.

Tom gave all his personal and company matters to ABC. He was going to switch law firms simply because Beth had chosen a proven law firm in the family law arena. So, Tom interviewed Arthur Gopple, the firm's litigation man. He had been with the firm for over 20 years and had a good reputation for all civil matters.

However, he lacked experience in the family law specialty. Tom grew uncomfortable with Arthur over the summer. Arthur recommended that he instruct the accountant to turn over the tax returns. Tom did not want to disclose the returns as they would reveal too much information about the business's success. Tom was right. Once the information was on the table, Tom thought he was doomed to pay an exorbitant amount as a settlement.

Arthur was the type of litigator who always tried to work out a deal rather than fight to ends of the earth. However, Arthur was not shy of fighting; he thought he would be doing a disservice to the client if he were to encourage Tom to fight on every point, and if he lost, appeal the ruling.

Tom approached his personal lawyer, Jeff Stands, at ABC. Together they went back and forth as to staying with the firm or going elsewhere. Jeff had known Tom almost from the beginning; a struggling entrepreneur who had the drive to succeed. Jeff also knew Beth.

While not on the same level of friendship, Jeff and his wife, Tom, and Beth usually met 2 or 3 times a year on a social basis while Jeff was preserving the account. Ultimately after a back-and-forth debate about Arthur's philosophy and his advice, Jeff conceded and told Tom to look to another lawyer outside his office for assistance following judgment.

Tom was a straight-shooter. He came down to the office and met with Arthur. He told Arthur that he was a good lawyer, but not the type of lawyer he wanted for the case. Tom told him that he could not afford to lose in the split up with Beth. Arthur understood. While he was disappointed, he knew that he had to protect the business account with ABC as it provided good legal work over the years. Arthur graciously said:

"Tom, I understand. Let me suggest that you retain Tim Harrigan. I have had a number of cases against him. He is a worthy litigator. I can continue to be a bouncing board for you. Let me know, and I will contact him for an appointment."

"Arthur, you are gentleman. I think that's good advice. I will take you up on this. So, send me a bill for the time to date. Thanks again, Arthur."

Tom met with Tim Harrigan a few days later. Tim Harrigan advised Tom to turn over the tax returns and other information requested. Tim advised him that he was going to lose on the support orders and eventually lose on the division of property.

What Tim did say, however, was there was going to be fight over the amount of support, the length of time to pay it, and the division of assets. Tom could not believe the advice he was getting from Tim.

At first, Tom was ready to move on to another lawyer. Tom did not want to accept Tim's advice. It was the same advice Arthur Gopple had given. Tom paused. He thought both lawyers can't be wrong. Reluctantly, Tom accepted Tim's advice. Tom dismissed Arthur, his lawyer throughout interim motions, but retained Tim Harrigan to defend him after the interim order.

Finally, September 15 arrived. Beth's case was number 1 on the list. But first, the court had to deal with adjournments, contested adjournments, and consent matters. All these cases took time; another 1.5 hours of lawyers' jousting for adjournments and consent orders. But now the Judge was ready at 2 PM for the hearing between Beth and Tom over, first, whether Beth needs support and second, if so, how much.

Court Hearing

"Ms. Matthews, please present your case."

Heidi presents Beth's case.

"Your Honour, Beth Richardson is the spouse of Thomas Richardson. They have been separated since August 2008, for almost 2 years without support. They have 2 children, ages 20 and 24 who are not financially independent. One child is interning at local hospital; the other child was in the business with Mr. Richardson.

"Mrs. Richardson has worked part-time at the family business, an advertising agency that photographs items for sale at retail stores and online. Prior to the separation, Beth was earning $9,000 a month plus benefits. She has not received a dollar since August 2008 despite interim orders in January 2009 and March 2010.

"Mrs. Richardson is presently unemployed and generally unemployable. She has no special training or skills that would give her the opportunity of earning at least $5,000 a month.

"Mrs. Richardson is presently living in rental condominium in central Toronto. Unfortunately, when the couple split, Thomas Richardson stopped paying the mortgage payments and utility bills. Consequently, the Canadiana Bank which held a first mortgage on the family home took judicial sale proceedings. The likelihood of Mrs. Richardson collecting any equity is remote.

"In short, Your Honour, Mrs. Richardson is now living substantially in a lower standard of living than she was before the separation. Beth's mother and friends are presently assisting her with the monthly rent and groceries."

"What do you want, Ms. Matthews?" says the judge.

"I want an order that Thomas Richardson pays Beth Richardson $9,000 a month from August 2008 to the present, her costs on a full amount basis, and $10,000 a month going forward. Mr. Richardson has been in breach of two earlier interim orders requiring him to pay $3,000 monthly. He has not paid anything. Both orders are under appeal, Your Honour."

"Have you looked at Mr. Richardson's financial information, Ms. Matthews?" said the Judge.

"Yes, Your Honour."

"What makes you think he can make these payments? He has not been working for over 1 year as a result of the firearms incident. He is collecting employment insurance of less than $2,000 a month. According to his statement of assets, he has no income to pay your client."

"Your Honour, if I may have your indulgence for a moment."

"Would you like a short recess to speak to your client?"

"Yes, Your Honour."

"OK, this Court will take a 10-minute break."

"Everyone, please rise," says the court Registrar.

The Judge stands and leaves through the back door.

"Well," says Tim to Heidi. "What do you want to do? We can agree on a number or you can continue with the judge and gamble that he does not dismiss your motion. Take a couple of minutes to discuss this with Mrs. Richardson."

Tim approaches Tom. "Tom, are you amenable to a number? You heard the Judge. He may dismiss her motion or award a smaller amount given your financial circumstances."

"What do you think, Tim? Should I offer $3,000 a month, no retroactive amounts?"

"That looks like a fair amount. However, Tom, please note that if Beth agrees, there is no appeal. Do I have your instructions to offer $3,000?"

"Yes. But if she refuses, no deal. No counteroffer. I want to leave the door open for an appeal."

Tim approaches Heidi and offers $3,000 a month, no arrears. Heidi then confers with Beth. Within seconds, Beth says, "No f—king way."

The court reconvenes.

The Judge says, "Ms. Matthews, have you had a chance to confer with your client?"

"Yes, Your Honour."

"What would you like to do?"

"I would like to continue arguing for monthly support payments of $9,000."

More discussion takes place with His Honour and Ms. Matthews, Ms. Matthews taking the position that Mr. Richardson's monthly income is more than what is listed on his statement of affairs.

Ms. Matthews raises the facts that:

- Tom had RRSPs and they are now gone;
- Tom had a substantial interest in the company and that interest is nowhere to be seen;
- Tom's trust had a second mortgage on the family home and after the Canadiana Bank sold it, the trust received its mortgage money.

These assets were now gone. Where they are today, no one knows except Tom.

Tim stands and responds, "Your Honour, I will be brief. Your Honour asked most of the questions that I had in mind.

"According to the statement of affairs, Tom has NO assets and limited cash-flow from Employment Insurance. In addition, Tom has not recovered from the shooting to the extent that he can travel for business. He is confined to Toronto if, as and when, he can work. His business is but gone. He works part-time for other agencies. In effect, Your Honour, his own business is dead.

"I submit Your Honour that Mrs. Richardson's motion be dismissed. Alternatively, Your Honour, her motion should be adjourned for one year to give Mr. Richardson time to heal and get back to work."

"Any reply, Ms. Matthews?"

"No, Your Honour. Counsel, you know that I must consider the Spousal Support Advisory Guidelines. Having regard to the length of the marriage, Mrs. Richardson's age at the time of the separation, her status as a homemaker to two children and her lack of training and skills, and having regard to Mr. Richardson's income over the last 3 years, his incapacity to regenerate substantial income, I have come to the conclusion that a support order requiring him to $9,000 monthly is unrealistic."

Noise erupts in the courtroom. Subdued cheers on Tom's side and boos and ohs on Beth's side.

"Quiet, please. Counsel, I intend to give reasons. I order that Mr. Richardson pay $2,000 monthly starting on the first day of each month for a total of 24 payments, starting 6 months from now."

Beth was again demoralized. Her situation went from bad to worse.

Round Two

The Judge left the door open for another appeal. The Judge failed to say how he arrived at that number and failed to give reasons as to why the support payments should start in 6 months.

Six months came and passed. Tom defaults in payments.

By this time, Tom's appeal had been perfected. Tom was ready for another court hearing. Beth's cross-appeal was ready. Beth maintained that Tom has the money, but refuses to pay. Beth maintained that Tom continues to live a good lifestyle without having to work.

Tim had cautioned Tom that too many hearings, too many appeals may be detrimental to his overall case. In fact, in some cases, the appeal court could increase the amount rather than overturning the award.

Tim encouraged Tom to make a deal. While such deals were unappealable if the parties consented, at least the parties knew what was expected. But that's what Tom didn't want. He wanted to stretch out hearings to the point where Beth would go away.

Appeal Court

The appeal from Judge White took place at Osgoode Hall, the home of the Appeal Court, the Divisional Court, and the Law Society of Ontario.

At 10:30, the 3 judges enter the courtroom. Counsel and other spectators rise. The Registrar reads the case name, and then Tim Harrigan stands and opens his presentation.

Tim reviews the record outlining that the motion court judge erred in determining the amount and when it should be paid.

"Unfortunately," says Tim, "the motion court Judge did not give reasons as the amount having regard that Mr. Richardson was presently unable to work and had limited income."

He added that his client is prepared to pay something but not at this time.

The president of the court leaned over to whisper to the Judge on his right and then leaned over to the Judge on the left.

"Ms. Matthews, we do not need to hear from you."

The president of the court then said, "We are going to dismiss the appeal. We are going to allow the cross-appeal by Mrs. Richardson and send it back to the trial court for another hearing. We will recess for 30 minutes while we prepare reasons."

Thirty minutes later, the court resumes.

The president then addresses counsel.

"We have concluded that Mr. Richardson has failed to disclose sufficient information and documents relating to his assets. While we have reviewed his tax returns for the last several years, we have concluded that his net income has been restructured.

"However, as we do not have full disclosure from Mr. Richardson, we cannot impute the sum of $10,000 per month to Mr. Richardson. If, in the future, Mr. Richardson produces more information, then the trial court can re-consider the amount that is being attributed to him.

"For the time being, we have decided to make the monthly payment of $5,000. However, such payments will not start until earlier of Mr. Richardson returning to work or 1 year from today. In the meantime, Mrs. Richardson is free to enforce this judgment."

Six months later, after another full hearing to determine Tom's income, the court re-affirms the $5,000 award until Mrs. Richardson can produce evidence of Tom's higher earnings. Once again Beth obtains an order that cannot be enforced. Once again, that order is under appeal.

Chapter Eight
Next Round One

As Heidi leaves the courtroom with Beth on September 15, she calls Arnold Jones on her cell phone. "Arnold, are you there, it's Heidi. We won! We won! Congratulations. The Judge confirmed the order that Tom to pay Beth $5,000 a month starting in November and directed another hearing to determine if the amount should be increased. That's fantastic. Don't you think?"

Arnold paused. He quelled. His partner had come through with a major victory for Beth and the firm.

Beth was delighted. But it took 13 court attendances and a year and half before a judge finally made a decision. "Why did it take so long?" said Beth.

Beth really did not understand, nor did anyone tell her that it would take so much time to resolve these issues.

"Why does it take so long? Why does it take so long?" she said first to herself and then to Heidi. "How did the Judge arrive at $5,000 a month? Why didn't the Judge award more? Does the Judge have guidelines? Is there a law on this? What does the law state?"

More questions for Heidi.

Heidi said, "One at a time. I can't answer all these questions today. It would take too long, and even then, I can't answer these questions directly. I would have to do some research. I may not find anything in the books. In the end, it was one Judge who took the initiative and then made a 'judgment call'."

"What does that mean?" said Beth.

"Well, there's no set formula for cases like this. However, there are guidelines. The Judge has the information supplied by Tom's lawyer and information that I gave the Judge on your behalf, and then the Judge makes a decision. The Judge has the discretion to make whatever order the Judge seems appropriate. However, as I said, there are some guidelines, but not a prescribed formula. It's all at the Judge's discretion, something that cannot be laid out in black-and-white terms."

Heidi could not answer her. Heidi would not have expected that it would take so long to get one Judge to order him to pay.

Now, Beth could start paying some of the bills coming in, including Heidi's bill which was already over the $35,000 mark.

"Not to spoil your win," says Heidi, "but Tom can appeal this decision."

"What? You've got to be kidding," says Beth. "You're telling me that after all this time, Tom can appeal this decision."

"Yes. When can you come into the office," said Heidi. "I have to speak to you about the next steps including preparing for an appeal. It's going to take about 2 hours. How's next Tuesday at 10?"

"Fine," said Beth. "And congratulations to you. Thank you."

Beth had the air let out of her victory balloon. She won, but she didn't win. Beth thought about where she was going with all of this. She knew Tom had employed the best of lawyers; she knew Tom didn't want to pay a penny if he didn't have to; she knew Tom had moved on in his life, and rest assured, Beth was not going to part of that. Beth was ready to give up.

Heidi calls Beth Monday morning. Heidi tells Beth that Tom has decided to appeal the judge's decision. Another appeal.

Silence on the phone.

Then, Beth says, "what does that mean?"

Heidi responds, "Tom has a 30-day window to appeal the ruling. His lawyer notified me this morning that Tom intends to appeal. The appeal will not be heard for many months as Tom has to prepare the appeal papers and then serve them to me so that I can reply. This all takes time. I'm sorry, Beth."

"Is there anything we can do before the appeal is heard?"

"It may be possible to bring an interim motion to the court requesting that Tom pay something on account while the appeal process takes place. I suggest that we take a look at this more carefully."

"How am I to live without any income?" says Beth. "I live in this home but have not paid for the water, the gas, and the electricity for months. God knows what the mortgage arrears are. They are going to cut me off soon, all of them. I am going to be evicted."

"You should be looking for a new home, a condo for example, or an apartment. Is there anyone who could help you financially? A relative? A friend?"

Beth was visibly upset. Her head down, tears were pouring down her face. Apart from some administrative duties, Beth had no particular skills or knowledge where she could obtain a decent-paying job. Beth had to find a home and a job to keep her going.

On the other hand, Heidi was becoming alarmed about the costs. Her accounts were not being paid and were in substantial arrears. Heidi's salary was dependent on her billings and the collection of her accounts. Heidi and the firm were fast becoming partners in Beth's case against Tom. Her employers were about to pull the plug on supporting Beth.

Beth's case was up for review by the management team. They would decide both Heidi's and Beth's fate at the next management meeting. With Tom appealing the $5,000 a month ruling, there would not likely be any results for well over another year. Could the firm stick with the case?

Fortunately for Heidi, the management team decided to carry Beth's case to the appeal stage, but the team refused to authorize Heidi to take any interim measure to collect. That motion would add another $20,000 bill to Beth's account. While Beth was not pleased with the decision not to bring an interim motion, she understood that she had received substantial services without paying for them. She thanked Heidi for standing by her during this interval.

The Appeal

Nine months later, Tom's lawyer, Tim Harrigan, delivers the appeal books to Heidi. Heidi spends another $10,000 in time preparing responding materials. Heidi's materials read well. She set out in chronological format the history of this family law fight. The weight was on the side of Beth. Tim Harrigan had an uphill fight.

With the emotional side on Beth, Heidi was reasonably confident the Judge would throw out the appeal without her being called to reply. That's not common, except where the court wants to hear from the other side on a particular point.

In July, the court sets October 9, the day after Thanksgiving, for the hearing of the appeal. Heidi prepares for the appeal the weekend before Labour Day.

As Heidi reviews her materials, she receives an email from Tim Harrigan. As she reads his email, her mouth opens aghast.

"Wow," Tim Harrigan wrote Heidi to inform him that his instructions are to abandon the appeal. That meant that the $5,000 award granted by Justice Martine was now final and could be enforced without restriction.

Great news for Heidi and Beth. Obviously, Tom must have thought, and Tim Harrigan must have advised, that his case was 50/50 at best and with the likelihood that he would lose. Tom must have realized that the court was going to award something to Beth; the only real issue was "How much?" His risk was that the court could increase the award from the motion court Judge.

So, from Tom's point of view, he bought another year and half and he increased Beth's legal costs to the point where her lawyers were ready to bail out of this case. That would be good news for Tom.

Heidi: "Let's schedule next Tuesday for a meeting."

Meeting—Tuesday at 10:00 at Heidi's Office

Heidi greets Beth at the reception and escorts her to the meeting room down the hall. They both sit down at the boardroom table.

"Would you like a coffee? Or tea?"

"Yes, coffee with a little milk would be fine. Thank you."

Heidi picks up the phone, calls, and requests 3 coffees. Just then, Sue Rodeo comes into the boardroom.

"'Sue' is a recent call to the bar and has joined our firm in the family dispute department. Sue is going to help with the enforcement of the support order."

"What do you mean she is going to help on the enforcement side? I don't understand."

"Just because the Judge ordered Tom to pay $5,000 monthly doesn't mean that he is going to pay."

"I don't understand. Didn't the judge make an order?"

"Yes, he did. But that doesn't mean he is going to pay."

This was beyond Beth's realm of thinking.

"I am married to this man for 24 years, now in divorce proceedings, and you tell me he may not pay."

"Yes, that's correct. He may not pay."

"I need the money. You know that. Where do you go from here?"

As the coffees are being brought in, Heidi starts on a short recital of Ontario law.

"You know, Beth, the law in Ontario gives you a choice of how you can proceed once a spouse obtains a support order. You have a choice: you can continue to retain me as your lawyer or you can enlist in the family support plan which is funded by the Ontario government. The system is enforced by government lawyers and paralegals at no expense to any support creditor. It's called the FRO for short, or the Family Responsibility Office.

"However, it is a government enforcement department so that you should not expect the same type of service as you may expect from an independent law firm. While there are good lawyers at FRO, they may not be up to your expectations. It's going to take up to 6 months for the FRO to start the case. You will have to meet with one of their representatives and go over the case in some detail.

"On the other hand, you can choose to stay with our firm and me, but it could get pricy with no guarantees on collection. Right now, your account is in arrears well over $55,000."

"Heidi, you know the case better than anyone. You have been with me from the start. For me to start changing lawyers does not make sense even though there is no fee. As long as you can continue to support me, I'm going to stay with you, Heidi."

"Thank you, Beth, for the vote of confidence. You should know that my firm expects to get paid for whatever you collect. We have to be first on the collection as the accounts are in arrears. The non-payment also affects my salary here and puts me at risk of not becoming a partner. I have worked many years here at this firm, and I can't jeopardize my position. Do you understand?"

"OK, you get the first moneys from the collection. But can we put a cap on the number? I need the money too. I need to buy groceries for myself and Rick; I need to pay rent, now that I have lost my home; and I need to buy some new clothes. I have not purchased a new dress for years let alone go to a ladies' salon to have my hair styled. Can we fix an amount?"

"Let me talk to Arnold. I'll get back to you."

"Now, let me briefly review the options. There are a number of ways to collect the money if Tom does not pay. The first and most important one is your right to examine Tom under oath as to his assets. This takes place at an official examiner's office. I'm there; you may choose to attend and listen; Tom is there with or without his lawyer; and the official examiner who takes down every word during the examination.

"You should know what he owns. We already have his financial statements. Those are the ones the Judge used in determining the amount that he should pay. Once we can identify an asset, we can instruct the sheriff to seize it, like a bank account. Hopefully, Tom will cooperate."

"I don't know what Tom owns. For that matter, I don't know what I own. We lived in this beautiful home in North York, drove 2 not so old cars, managed to send both children to university debt free. I know he has some savings in the form of RRSPs and has a gold coin collection that he keeps in the safe. That's it—No, he has the business where I receive a salary for part-time administration. I suppose he owns the business."

"OK, fasten your seat belt. Hopefully, this will be a short roll-a-coaster ride. Perhaps, we will get lucky within the next 6 months. Once Tom starts paying, you will be OK until there is a change in financial circumstances. With your instructions, I will begin to set up an official examination for Tom. Do you understand?"

"Yes, please proceed."

The meeting finishes. Heidi tells Sue to remain in the boardroom and then escorts Beth to the elevators.

Little did Beth know what she was in for. She was not ready for a long ride on a roll-a-coaster with no end in sight.

Heidi returns to the boardroom and sits down.

Instructions to Sue.

"Sue, it's one thing to get a judgment, it's another to collect. From what Beth has told me over the last 3 years and during the course of this file, Tom is going to do everything not to pay. This should be a great exercise for you.

"First, I want you to read up about collecting debts. There are good texts on creditor and debtor rights and remedies. Once you have completed this, make sure that you read some case law, especially on judgment debtor examinations or more formally, the examination in aid of execution. There are some good precedents from the Bar Admission Course.

"Sue, do you understand? Do you have any questions?"

"When do you want this?"

"Yesterday"—pause—"Our firm is owed a lot of money for unpaid fees. We need to expedite the collection if we are going to get paid. Next, we have to serve Tom with a notice of examination. You can prepare that and arrange with Right Process, our court service provider, to serve the notice on Tom.

"Make sure you give them Tom's new address and his business address. I'm sure he will duck service at least the first time. Tom's got an excellent lawyer who will put obstacles in your way. So, get ready, Sue. Please prepare the notice of examination and the questionnaire."

Judgment Debtor Examination December 10

Sue has done her homework. She read the leading text on creditors and debtors and some case law on judgment debtor examinations. She prepared the notice of examination returnable on December 10 and then made arrangements for Right Process to serve Tom as soon as possible. She ran this by Heidi and they were ready to go. Right Process reported that they had served Tom on November 15 and forwarded an affidavit of service.

Beth was naive to think that once the Judge gave her judgment, Tom would be ready to pay. Not so. Beth was in for a fight of her life, and she didn't know it. Heidi's process server served Tom with an appointment to examine him in aid of execution returnable on December 10.

As explained to Beth, it is one thing to get a judgment, and something else to get paid. What Heidi didn't tell Beth was that she was likely beginning a long and expensive road to nowhere. Tom had been forewarned and took steps to move his assets around so that they would not be able to be seized by the sheriff in satisfaction of the debt.

Heidi told her that one of the first ways to find assets was to examine him under oath. If the lawyer was able to identify an asset of some value, the lawyer could instruct the sheriff to seize it. Ultimately, if he couldn't find anything, she could always put him into bankruptcy as a last resort. That would affect his credit and make it more difficult for Tom to get a VISA or MASTER card or apply for a new car loan.

On the other hand, putting Tom into bankruptcy would give him a window to go back to the court and request a reduction in the support payments. If he is bankrupt, he would not have the income or assets to pay the arrears, let alone continue paying. Beth was on a teeter-totter, a see-saw: on the one side finding the assets to seize; on the other side, Tom's taking bankruptcy protection and applying to reduce support payments.

So, what was involved? Tom's examination was scheduled for December 10 at 10 in the morning. The examination was to take place at an official examiner's office located at 1 Ontario Street, suite 500. There are many such offices in downtown Toronto and elsewhere in the city for these types of examinations.

The actual office was within a larger office having multiple rooms for examinations. The examination room is about 10 x 15 feet, has a rectangular table with 7 chairs, 3 on each side, and the 7th at one end where the court reported sits. Most often, there is a window along the width of the room. On the 5th floor, there is not much to look out at except for other office towers.

In the expensive official examiner's offices, somewhere over 35 stories high, the examination room usually has a view of the lake, the GO trains, or the northern Toronto skyline. Needless to say, the costs are much higher all the way around: higher rent and higher examination rates. In this case, Heidi booked the least expensive examiner's office knowing that Heidi would have to pick up the fees as Beth did not have any money.

At the reporter's end is a dictating machine that records the voices of the participants. There are microphones set in front of each chair. The witness, Tom, sits closest to the reporter with his lawyer alongside.

In these examinations, so-called JDs or judgment debtor examinations, the debtor shows up with his or her lawyer more than a few minutes before the appointed time, and the lawyer for the creditor shows up with his or her associate or student to take separate notes. They help themselves to a cup of coffee or tea and some sort of fruit muffin. The real creditor rarely attends these examinations unless there is substantial amount of money involved.

JDs usually last about one to two hours. Over many years, the legal profession can readily obtain a long list of questions designed to flush out debtor's assets. Once discovered, the creditor's lawyer can then direct the sheriff of the county or district where the debtor resides or carries on business to seize the asset. Ordinarily, the creditor's lawyer does not order a copy of the transcript. It's expensive, a few thousand dollars or more, and the transcript is seldom needed later. This was no ordinary JD as Heidi was about to find out.

The reporter is trained to transcribe and record all discussions at the table except where the lawyers request that the reporter stop. This job can be most stressful for reporters as most often lawyers and their clients tend to over talk each other to the point where the reporter throws up his or her hands in frustration and yells, "Stop."

"I can't record what is being said if both of you are talking at the same time."

When the witness appears, the reporter asks the witness to swear under the Old or New Testament or Koran that he or she will tell the truth. If the witness is non-religious, the reporter requests the witness declare or affirm that he or she will answer the questions honestly and truthfully.

9:50. Heidi, Sue, and Beth arrive at the examiner's office, check in with the receptionist. They are escorted down the hall to the designated examination room, Room 210. They stop first for a cup of coffee and proceed to the examination room.

Heidi introduces herself to the reporter and gives the reporter a copy of the judgment and her professional card for identification. Heidi then introduces Sue and then Beth. They sit down and wait for Tom and his lawyer to appear. Heidi opens her valise, takes out her notes, some pencils, some documents, her questionnaire, and post-its. The reporter sets up the recorder, tests the microphones, makes notes as to who is present and in what capacity.

10:00. Tom does not appear.

10:15. Tom does not appear. Heidi, Sue, and Beth continue to engage in social talk, the weather, and from time to time, chat about nothing in particular.

"Where the Hell is he?" Heidi pulls out her phone and calls Tim Harrigan. No answer.

Heidi leaves him a voicemail that she is in the examination room, but Tom failed to appear. Heidi then sends a text to Tim. "Where are you?"

No reply.

10:30. Heidi and Beth look at each other. Beth says, "What's going on? Why isn't he here?"

Heidi didn't know the answers. All she could do was wait until she could contact Tim Harrigan.

10:45. Heidi, Sue, and Beth decide to leave. Heidi requests that the reporter record her opening address. Heidi states for the record that, "My name is Heidi Matthews. I am at the official examiner's office with my client, Beth Richardson. We appeared for the examination in aid of execution of Thomas Richardson at 10 AM on December 10, but that the defendant Thomas

Richardson failed to show up by 10:45. I also add that I attempted to contact Thomas Richardson's lawyer, Tim Harrigan, by text and telephone, but Tim Harrigan did not respond to either communication."

At 10:48, Heidi and Beth leave. Heidi requests that the reporter issue a certificate of non-attendance. The reporter confirms and says that she will put one in the mail to her office. Heidi knows that she needs a certificate of non-attendance just in case Tom does this again. Sometimes, these certificates are used on motions to compel the defendant to appear failing which the court can issue a contempt order. Heidi knows to have these certificates on hand just in case.

Beth is depressed. She expected that Tom would appear and go through the examination identifying assets that the sheriff could seize, especially the bank accounts.

Heidi meanwhile consoles Beth and heads back to her office. She reports to Arnold that Tom failed to show. Arnold smirks. He knows the games that debtors can play. Arnold suggests that Heidi call Tim Harrigan this afternoon and find out what's going on.

Nothing is going on. She calls Tim's office again. This time Tim answers.

"Where were you?" says Heidi. "I have been sitting at the examiners for the last hour, and your client failed to show."

"Stop," says Tim. "Tom retained a new lawyer last week. I don't know his name or firm. The new lawyer was supposed to contact you."

The call ended abruptly.

Judgment Debtor Examination April 9

Heidi's paralegals serve Tom again with a notice of examination scheduled for April 9 at 10 in the morning. Heidi, Sue, and Beth show up at about 9:50 on April 9. They are escorted down to another examination room. They sit down facing the inside wall. The reporter asks the same questions. "Can I have a copy of the judgment? Who is appearing for whom?"

Heidi does the introductions again. "I am the lawyer for Beth Richardson, the judgment creditor; this is Sue Rodelo, also a lawyer at our firm and this is Ms. Beth Richardson."

The reporter leaves the room with a copy of the judgment to photocopy and returns just before 10. Heidi opens her briefcase and spreads her notes on the table. Heidi has a 16-page questionnaire that Sue prepared for her.

Heidi, Sue, and Beth wait. It's 10:15. Heidi turns to Beth and says, "He's one son of bitch. He is doing this again."

Just then, Heidi's phone rings. She cannot identify the caller. She answers anyway.

"Ms. Matthews, yes."

"This is Macy Schwabas. I have been retained by Tom Richardson to attend with him at his examination. I'm sorry that we are late."

"OK," replies Heidi. "When can we expect you?"

"It would be great if we could re-schedule the appointment?" Macy expecting that she would agree.

"No. We will wait for you."

"OK," he replied. "We are stuck on the Yonge University subway line. The TTC announced an emergency at the Davisville Station and that they would be sending buses. We don't know when we will arrive."

"We will wait," replied Beth.

11:30 came and passed. 12:00 came and passed. Heidi calls Macy Schwabas. He answers. He says he is on the bus with Tom Richardson at the Bloor Street station. It may take another hour.

Heidi, now totally frustrated, and calls him back. "Let's re-schedule. It's 12:30. Can you bring him tomorrow?"

Macy replies, "I'll have to check with my office." Pause.

Macy checks his phone calendar. "No, I don't think so. Let's book a date in early June after the Victoria Day holiday. I have to check my diary again."

Heidi reluctantly agrees. "I'll call your office this afternoon to book another date."

In the meantime, Heidi makes a short statement as before and then asks the reporter for another certificate of non-attendance. Heidi and Beth leave the official examiner's office.

On returning to the office, Heidi repeats the story to Arnold. He shrugs this time. How often does this happen? For the educated debtor, it happens a lot. Debtors delay in facing reality. Some debtors do it out of spite. Other debtors are so carefree they don't know they are causing a stir and blood pressure to rise. And some debtors are so well-educated, they always seem to be under the radar.

Heidi calls Macy Schwabas in mid-afternoon and books June 14 at 10 for two hours. Heidi tells Mr. Schwabas that she now has two certificates of nonattendance, and if Tom Richardson fails to appear on June 14, she had instructions to move for an order compelling him to attend.

Heidi calls Beth and tells her to keep June 14 open. Beth is depressed. She has no money. She has not paid Heidi; she has not paid the rent on her apartment; she has not paid any of the utilities; she has maxed out on her credit cards for groceries.

She knows Tom well. Tom will do everything to avoid paying, let alone being examined.

Judgment Debtor Examination June 14

June 14, Heidi, Sue and Beth show up at the official examiner's office by 10. They go through the same routine of introductions and identification. They walk down to Room 298. Heidi lays out her notes and questionnaire. At 10, Tom Richardson and Macy Schwabas appear.

"Hello, my name is Macy Schwabas. Which one of you is Heidi Matthews?"

Heidi sticks out her hand to shake and Macy graciously shakes her hand.

Tom says hello to both. Macy introduces himself to Sue and sits down at one of the chairs.

Macy says to Tom, "No, don't sit there. Sit over there beside the reporter facing the inside wall."

Macy wanted Tom to face the inside of the room as often witnesses tend to gaze out and lose their focus on answering questions while looking out of the window. Macy had some experience defending debtors.

"OK. Is everyone ready," announces the reporter.

"Who is testifying today?"

"Tom Richardson."

"Has he been sworn in?"

The reporter proceeds to administer the oath to Tom.

"Mr. Richardson, please stand up." She presents him with a Holy Bible. "Do you promise to tell the truth, the whole truth, and nothing but the truth, so you help you, God?"

Tom interrupts, "I prefer not to swear on the bible."

Beth leans over to Heidi's ear, "Tom has always been religious. What's he doing?"

The reporter notes that and changes the oath to "Do you solemnly affirm, to tell the truth, the whole truth and nothing but the truth?"

Tom says, "I do." Tom has been counseled; he has been prepped for this examination; he is ready.

Macy and Tom met the day before the examination date at Macy's office. They discussed the procedure and Macy gave Tom some basic rules on a sheet of paper. These include:

- Tell the truth.
- Answer the question directly when you can.
- Answer with a Yes or a No.
- If you are asked for an explanation, keep it short, very short.
- If you do not know, say so.
- Do not guess.

"Take this sheet home and memorize the rules, but don't bring the sheet to the examination. OK?"

Tom says he understands.

Heidi starts.

"What is your name?"

"Tom Richardson."

"Do you have a middle name?"

"Yes."

"Why didn't you tell me when I asked for your name?"

"You didn't ask me."

"Do you have a middle name?"

"I don't use my middle name."

"What is it?"

"Ivan."

"Is Tom your nickname?"

"Yes."

"What is your proper first name?"

"Thomas."

"Are you the judgment debtor in these proceedings?"

"What proceedings are you referring to?"

Heidi shows Tom a copy of the judgment. "Are you shown her as the defendant?"

"Yes."

Heidi says to the reporter, "Please make the judgment exhibit 1."

Heidi takes the stamp and affixes it to the copy of the judgment, and then fills in the date and case name.

Heidi produces the notice of examination.

"Do you recognize this?"

"Yes."

"You were served with a copy of this notice for December 10, were you not?"

"Yes."

"Did you appear on December 10?"

"No."

"Why not?"

"My lawyer quit on me."

"You were served with a copy of this notice for April 9, were you not?"

"Yes."

"Did you appear on April 9?"

"No."

"Why not?"

"I was stuck in traffic with my new lawyer, Mr. Schwabas."

"Ms. Reporter, please make the two notices Exhibit 2 to this examination." Heidi marks the notices.

"Now, Mr. Richardson, did you read the notices?"

"I glossed over them."

"Did you read them?"

"I didn't understand a lot of the words, you know, they are technical legal words."

"Did you bring any of the documents listed on the back?"

"No."

"Why not?"

"There are too many documents. I did not have time to retrieve them all, and I wanted to bring them all together."

"Will you produce them?"

"If I can find them."

"When?"

"As soon as I can assemble them?"

"When is that?"

"As I said, as soon as I can assemble them."

Heidi: "Give me a date."

"No, I can't do that. I do not know how long it will take."

"Why not? You have had these notices for several months."

"I will have to speak to my accountant, to my lawyer, and office staff. Many of the documents are stored in boxes at a warehouse. It will take time to get them."

"Well, Mr. Richardson, you have had since December to produce these documents, and to date, today, June 14, you have not produced one document."

"Ms. Matthews, if I may interrupt."

"No. You cannot interrupt. This is my examination. I want an answer from him, not you."

"Ms. Matthews, I have just been retained. I have not had sufficient time to review these notices with my client. I suggest you give us a couple of months to assemble documents."

Pause.

"OK, you have until August 31. If we do not have the documents by then, we will be moving for a contempt order. Let's book the date now."

"Thank you, Ms. Matthews."

"Let's continue with the examination, Mr. Schwabas. I don't need the documents for my questions."

"What is your salary from the company? I am showing you a salary stub for last year."

"I don't know. I haven't received a salary for many months."

"How many months?"

"I don't know."

"Give me an approximate number."

"Ms. Matthews, I don't think it's fair to put questions to Mr. Richardson without his having the opportunity to review the document. You're asking him to guess. To be clear, I have instructed him to refuse answering questions where he has to guess. So, I suggest we adjourn this examination until a date after August 31. Is that OK?"

Ms. Matthews requests a short 5-minute break to discuss this with her client.

Heidi and Beth go out into the hall. Heidi says that if she continues to ask questions, Mr. Schwabas will continue to tell Tom not to answer. In short, we have a stand-off. We could take this line and apply to the court for a ruling. But that is going to take more time and more costs.

"I recommend that we give them the adjournment. Do you agree?"

Beth reluctantly nods in favour of the adjournment.

After a few minutes of standing in the hall, Ms. Matthews returns and agrees to fix the next examination date for October 15.

"Let me check with my office."

Pause. Mr. Schwabas calls his office and speaks to his assistant. He clears October 15.

Mr. Schwabas agrees. And everyone leaves.

Judgment Debtor Examination October 15.

Same setup, same review.

Macy Schwabas and Tom Richardson show up at 10:10.

The reporter looking at Mr. Richardson says, "You are still sworn for this session."

Macy says, "Good morning, Ms. Matthews. Good morning Mrs. Richardson. I have Mr. Richardson's summary tax returns for the last 3 years. I do not have the RRSPs statements, nor the insurance policies. I do not have the deeds for the business property and some of the other documents you requested.

"Unfortunately, Aero Warehousing misplaced the corporation's files after a smoke detector triggered the sprinkler systems in mid-May. They told us that they had to move files and cartons around to avoid further water damage."

"Here's Mr. Dolman's telephone number," handing her a post-it with a name and number.

"He is the operations manager at Aero Warehousing. He said it's going to take months to find Mr. Richardson's company files as he is being pressured by other tenants to retrieve their files. Please contact him directly to find out more information. I'm sorry. But there's not much we can do."

"That's terrible," said Heidi. "It seems that we're not accomplishing very much." Heidi lets out a sigh of frustration.

“Let’s take a look at the tax returns. Where are the schedules?”

“What schedules? These are his summaries.”

“No, no, Mr. Schwabas. Where are the schedules?”

“The summaries have all the information you need,” said Mr. Schwabas.

“Since when are you telling what I need,” said Heidi. “I wanted the full tax return for the last 3 years. Will you produce them?”

Heidi says to the reporter, “Did you get all this?”

The reporter nods yes.

“Mr. Schwabas, you have produced 3 summary tax returns, and no other documents according to the notice of examination. You have advised that there was water damage in early May at the warehouse where the personal and corporate records are stored and that you have been unable to locate your client’s files. Is this correct?”

“Yes and No. As I said, the personal and corporate records are stored at Aero Warehousing. These records are somewhere in the warehouse.”

“Mr. Richardson, let’s review the 2018 summary tax return.”

“Is this return correct?”

“I assume so.”

“What do you mean that you assume so?”

“Well, I didn’t prepare the return. Our company bookkeeper and accountant prepared the return.”

“Where did the information come from?”

“The bookkeeper and the accountant.”

“What are their names?”

Tom looks at Macy and says, “Do I have to tell them?”

Macy nods his head up and down.

Tom answers: “It’s Betty Wight and Chris Honest.”

“Where can I get a hold of them?”

“Betty works part-time at the business, and Chris is a partner at the firm of Honest, Arb, and James.”

“What was your net income before taxes in 2017?”

“35,678.00”

“What was your net income before taxes in 2018?”

“39,567.00”

“What was your net income before taxes in 2019?”

“41,456.00”

"Where do you live?"

"108 Great Tichfield Drive, Toronto."

"Who owns the home?"

"246800 Ontario Inc."

"Who owns 246800 Ontario Inc.?"

"The Tom Richardson Trust."

"What's the approximate value of the home?"

"I don't know."

"Is there a mortgage against the home?"

"Yes."

"Who holds the mortgage?"

"There is a first mortgage to the Canadiana Bank for about $2.5 million and a second mortgage to The Tom Richardson Trust II for $600,000."

"Will you produce the Canadiana Bank mortgage?"

Mr. Schwabus: "It's in the Aero Warehouse with the other documents. I don't know when we will be able to retrieve the original mortgage. Besides, Ms. Matthews, you can get a copy online. In fact, let me have a copy, and I undertake to pay for it. OK?"

Heidi replies, "It's still Mr. Richardson's responsibility to produce all the documents."

"What about the mortgage to The Tom Richardson Trust II?"

Mr. Schwabus replies, "What about it?"

Heidi says, "Will you produce that mortgage as well?"

Mr. Schwabus says, "I won't repeat myself. But it is the same answer."

"What's the house worth today?"

"I don't know."

"Is it worth $3 million?"

"I don't know."

"Is it worth $2 million?"

"I don't know."

"Why don't you know?"

"I am not in the real estate business."

"Can you give me an estimate?"

"No. I have no idea."

Heidi continues, "What are the monthly expenses?"

"I don't know," says Mr. Richardson.

"Why don't you know?" says Heidi.

"I don't pay the bills."

"Who does?"

"The bookkeeper."

"Will you provide a list of the bills she pays? I'm asking you, Mr. Richardson, will you provide a list of the bills?"

"I will speak to her."

"Thank you."

"When can you produce this information?"

"I don't know."

"How about by December 5?"

Tom: "I'll try."

"What's in the Tom Richardson Trust? What assets does it hold?"

"I don't know."

"What do you mean you don't know?"

"It was set up years ago by my then lawyers. I don't know what's in it. I don't manage it."

"Who does?"

"My bookkeeper and accountant."

"OK, let's adjourn this examination to a date in mid-January."

"How about January 24?"

"Sounds good today."

"Let's book it."

Judgment Debtor Examination January 24.

January 24 comes and goes.

Mr. Schwabus calls Heidi Mathews and advises that he has a conflict for January 24.

"Let's re-arrange the examination for April 15."

"OK," says Heidi. "But I am going to bring a motion to compel the bookkeeper and accountant to testify. Please give me some dates in April."

Heidi calls Beth and again tells her to be patient. Collections take time. Beth listens, but she is not responding. Beth puts down the phone and starts to cry.

"Where am I going with all of this," she says.

"He's beating Heidi to a pulp. She's no match for Mr. Schwabus."

After a few days, Beth decides to call Heidi and requests a meeting with her and Arnold Jones. March 1 at 2 PM is set for the meeting.

March 1, Meeting at Jones, Wilson

At the offices of Jones, Wilson, Beth meets with Heidi in the reception. They wait in the reception. Heidi knew this was serious as Beth called Arnold Jones directly, and requested the meeting with him. Arnold felt uncomfortable as he was not totally familiar with the case. Heidi had kept him informed generally, but she never gave the specifics. He knew however that there were large unpaid accounts.

"Good afternoon, Beth. Would you like a cup of coffee?" says Heidi.

"No thank you, Heidi. Please call Arnold. I would like to start the meeting if you don't mind," says Beth.

Heidi signals the receptionist to call Arnold and to tell him to meet Heidi and Beth in the 3rd meeting room. Heidi and Beth walk down the hall to the 3rd meeting room. Arnold stands at the door to greet Beth. In his hands, he has several pages of unpaid accounts. Heidi billed Beth after every examination date, and together with the costs of the support motion, Beth was indebted to Jones, Wilson for over $95,000 plus disbursements and taxes.

They sit down at the table. Heidi gives a short summary of the each of the examinations of Tom and says to Arnold, "We have very little information about Tom's assets. He produced only the summary pages of his tax returns. While they are informative, they do not give full particulars of income and disposition of capital assets. Tom has avoided or evaded producing information and documents.

"We do not have a strong case for a motion to compel him to answer nor the evidence in support of a motion to hold him in contempt. He has given one excuse after another to avoid answering. I would like to bring a motion compelling him to answer but I am afraid that if we win, he will appeal, and that appeal with take another 6 to 18 months for it to be heard.

"The bottom line in all this one more full year has passed since the support order was made and it will be another year and probably more time if we bring the motion. I also want to bring a motion to compel the bookkeeper and the accountant to testify. It seems that they have all the information."

Beth says, "I am losing confidence in my case. I have this order, but it is unenforceable. Heidi is doing her best, but Tom's new lawyer, Mr. Schwabas, is putting too many obstacles in our way."

Heidi says, "I would like to bring contempt proceedings against Tom."

"What if we lose?" says Beth. "If we lose, we appeal," answers Beth.

"No, no. I don't agree with both of you," says Arnold. "Either way, Beth loses. If she wins, he appeals; if she loses, she appeals. In both cases, there is an 18-month delay in getting information and documents. Beth needs the money now. We have unpaid legal bills!"

Arnold is now having second thoughts about taking on this case. As much as he wants to keep his lawyers busy, this case is not producing any money. Heidi's time may be written down or written off. Heidi does not know that yet, but if Arnold decides to withdraw from acting for Beth, Heidi's salary and perhaps her bonus are in jeopardy. These are tough cases for small and intermediate size law firms.

They take these cases in the anticipation of getting paid down the line. They are not like personal injury law firms where if the client has been injured, the client invariably wins in court or settles with the insurance company. Personal injury lawyers do well, especially where insurers are reluctant to go to court over deciding how much to pay out.

On the other hand, legal fees in questionable family law matters are usually hard fought and unless the family is wealthy, the chances of recovering such time are not great. Arnold now realizes that Tom Richardson has had some expert legal advice and has sheltered his assets to the point where Heidi or whoever Arnold chooses to continue the action would be put to the ultimate collection of a well-knowledgeable debtor and an excellent defence counsel.

Arnold wants a time-out. He is not sure whether to continue with Beth and take Heidi off the case and put in someone else. He is not sure he wants to stay with Beth. Arnold is in a lose, lose situation. Heidi will spend more time without reward. Heidi can't afford to bring a motion for contempt. Even if she wins, Tom will appeal. The more time passes, the more Arnold's firm loses as does Heidi in her salary.

What should Arnold do? Well, this decision had to be made by the management team, once again. Arnold meets with his partners on the first Monday of every month.

Arnold tells Beth that he can't make any decision right now, that he has to discuss the case with his partners and management team.

"Beth, I'm sorry right now. We can't go forward without my consulting the management team. Let's discuss this again in mid-August. Please call my office late in July for an appointment."

Arnold and Heidi lead Beth out of the board room to the reception area where she waits for the elevator.

Meeting with Joyce

Beth too is having second thoughts about staying with Heidi and Arnold. Not that Heidi is not doing her job, she is. It is Tom's lawyer that is making the collection most difficult and Beth has no money to pay for continued legal services.

Beth is depressed. She calls her good friend Joyce. Time to have lunch again and get caught up on the action.

Beth and Joyce meet again at the Yonge Street Diner at 11:30 on July 14. Beth is visibly upset. She has had second thoughts about Heidi and more than a whole year has gone by without any results, and $95,000 plus in unpaid legal fees. Beth is struggling to pay rent, food, and utilities. She has no income; she can't get a job; she is totally reliant on her parents who are aging and need money for home care.

They both ordered salad niçoise and two glasses of chardonnay. Joyce thinks she made a mistake by referring Beth to Jones, Wilson. She thinks she should have looked around for a more seasoned family law litigator. Of course, Joyce knows that with a more experienced person, the fees go up. Beth could hardly afford Jones, Wilson, let alone an experienced family law litigator.

What she needed was the support that is given to spouses who do not have the means to retain private lawyers. Joyce recalls at one of the earlier meetings that Arnold had mentioned that the Ontario government sponsored the collection of support orders at no cost to the support creditor.

Bingo! Arnold had spoken briefly about the Family Responsibility Office, commonly called the FRO. He described the office as a government office with government lawyers and paralegals whose sole function was to collect on support orders. While not demeaning the FRO, he said there is a difference between private enforcement and government enforcement. However, the support creditor did not have to pay anything, and that was the bonus to Beth.

Joyce empathizes with Beth. She knows what a terrible predicament she is in, and feels more badly by referring her to Jones Wilson. While they are good lawyers, they were not able to deal with Tom's lawyers. The judicial system moved too slowly and was too expensive. Joyce felt she made a better decision to refer Beth to the FRO. At least the expense was off the table.

The FRO

Having lost faith in the private enforcement, Beth turns to the FRO for help in September. She calls Heidi. Heidi is not available and Beth leaves a voicemail requesting Heidi call her. Heidi detects an issue as Beth's voice was quivering. Heidi guessed right. Beth was about to transfer the case to FRO, but she needed Heidi's input in filling out the forms. Heidi took a deep breath. She knew her salary was in danger this year as her income was significantly down. She was also concerned about being rejected as a future partner.

Beth calls for assistance. They refer her to the website and request that she complete an application for assistance. The application is a form that resembles all the information that Heidi tried to get from Tom. First, Beth has to supply a copy of the support order, her identification, and the steps that she has taken since the order was made.

Beth asks Heidi to assist and prepare the answers to the application. Once completed, Beth files the application with FRO by the end of October and waits about 30 days for a reply. After an agent reviews the form and asks more questions, Beth takes a number on the enforcement of the support order.

Tom completes his divestments of his interests.

Before Beth and Tom separated, Tom had sufficient assets to pay Beth $9,000 a month. What happened to those assets? Wondered Beth.

- Owner of the advertising business. Tom was the owner all right. But Beth did not know the details. Tom had 100% of the shares. Six years before the break-up, Tom transferred the shares to a family trust that was being administered by his good friend and lawyer, Jeff Stands. Tom was a discretionary beneficiary.
  The business borrowed $500,000 from the Canadiana Bank on the security of the business's receivables, its leasehold interest in the property on which the business was located, and Tom's personal

guarantee. Tom received $450,000 for his shares from his company at that time and the money soon disappeared into numbered company's bank account in the Bahamas.

- $160,000 in RRSPs. Tom began withdrawing $5,000 a month once he felt that his marriage was irreconcilable. By the time they were in court on the second round, the RRSPs had dropped well below $30,000.

- The family home at 108 Great Tichfield Drive, Toronto. It's owned by 246800 Ontario Inc. which in turn is owned by the Tom Richardson Trust. The property had two mortgages against it. The Ontario Bank held the first mortgage for $1,300,000 at 5% interest with monthly interest payments of $5,416.66.

  The second mortgage was held by The Tom Richardson Trust II, a private syndicate group. It was $600,000 at 7.5% with monthly interest payments of $3,750. As an owner, 246800 Ontario Inc. had to pay $9,166.66 monthly.

  Once they separated, Beth could not make the mortgage payments, and so the second mortgagee took over the home. Following the separation, Beth agreed to move out of the home as no one was paying the mortgages. Wendy was living in residence. Rick had the living room sofa.

Contempt Hearings

On January 3, some two years after the support order was made, Agent 657 of the FRO office notifies Tom that the FRO is now in charge of collection. Tom refers the Agent to his lawyer, Mr. Schwabas.

"Hello, Mr. Schwabus, this is Agent 657 of the Family Responsibility Office. Are you familiar with the FRO?"

"Yes, I am. Do you have a name Agent 657?"

"My name is Stanley Mah. Please address all correspondence to Agent 657. OK?"

"Are you a lawyer?"

"No. I am a paralegal. If this matter proceeds to court, FRO will assign a lawyer."

"What do you want?" says Macy Schwabas.

"I want all the documents set out in the notice of examination sent by Ms. Richardson's former law firm including full tax returns and income and expense statements for the last 12 months. Can you do that?"

"I'll see what I can do. I have not been involved in this matter for almost one year. I think I have to check to see if I am still retained. Is that OK?"

"Yes, can you let me know by the end of the week, and if you are still retained or retained again, please give me a date that I can expect to see the documents."

"OK."

Mr. Schwabas calls Agent 657 Friday afternoon. He leaves a voicemail to the effect that his retainer ran out and that Mr. Richardson advised that he would make an appointment to sign another retainer agreement and look into supplying the documents in a more timely manner.

Another two weeks pass. Agent 657 sends an email to Mr. Schwabus requesting the status of his retainer. Mr. Schwabus replies a couple of days later advising that he has not heard from Mr. Richardson and that he would follow up.

Macy Schwabas then hustles a new retainer agreement and deposit and tells Tom that he should produce as many documents as he can as soon as he can. Macy tells Tom that if he continues to delay, the FRO will bring a motion for an order compelling him to produce, and that is likely to happen. Tom sluffs off the threat, but in good faith signs the retainer and starts assembling all the paper.

Macy Schwabus and Agent 657 then arrange a mutually agreed date to examine Tom. The examination is set for August 8, well over two years since Tom's last examination.

At the same Official Examiner's office, Agent 657 shows up at 9:50 and is escorted to room 15 for the examination. Macy Schwabas and Tom arrive at 10:00. They walk down the hall to room 15. Beth is noticeably absent. Macy introduces himself and then Tom. The court reporter gives her introduction and then takes a copy of the judgment out of the room for photocopying. Agent 657 requests to see the documents.

Tom opens up his briefcase and pulls out the same documents he presented before Heidi.

"Where are the rest of the documents?" says Stanley Mah. "You have the notice of examination and you see the list of documents requested. Where are the full tax returns? Where are your income and expense statements for the last 12 months? Where are they?”

“Well, I don’t know where they are,” Tom starts to talk, but Macy interrupts him. “Mr. Richardson has not been able to obtain more documents. Whatever documents he has were misplaced in Aero Warehousing after a water flood. As explained to Ms. Matthews, Mrs. Richardson’s former lawyer, their sprinkler system went off causing a huge flood in the warehouse.

“Mr. Richardson has sued the Aero Warehouse for compensation for the loss of his personal and business records. They have defended and at the same time, they have, from what they have told us, that they retained computer specialists to reconstruct not only Mr. Richardson’s files but also the files of other tenants.”

“OK,” says Stanley Mah. “Let’s start the examination in any event.”

“Mr. Richardson, have you been sworn or affirmed?”

“Yes.”

“Yes, what? Have you been sworn?”

“No.”

“Have you been affirmed?”

“Yes.”

“Within the last 5 years, and now, does anyone or your company owe you money?”

“No.”

“Do you own shares of publicly traded companies?”

“Do you own shares in a private company?”

“No.”

“Do you have any government-sponsored savings accounts like RRSPs?”

“No.”

“Do you have any jewelry?”

“Just my watch.”

“What is the value?”

“It’s an old watch. It has no real value.”

“How much did it cost when you bought it?”

“$35.00.”

“Do you have any collections like stamps, coins, or wine?”

“No.”

“Do you have any horses or boats?”

"No, no."

"Do you have any interest in any:

- patent, copyright,
- process, formula,
- invention or royalties."

"No to all of the above."

"Do you have any life insurance?"

"No."

"Do you own any camera equipment?"

"No."

"Do you have any assets or money outside Canada?"

"No."

"Do you have any bank accounts? Credit union accounts?"

"No."

"Have you transferred any property over the value of $1,000 within the last 5 years?"

"No."

"Thank you, Mr. Richardson. I would like to adjourn this examination to the first week of October, say October 8 at 10:00 pending your delivering all the documents in the notice of examination. Do you think you can deliver them by September 8?"

"You have had ample time to produce them."

"Mr. Schwabas, do you agree? Are you available on October 8?"

"Yes, that sounds reasonable. I'll book October 8."

"Good, this examination is adjourned on consent to October 8, at 10:00."

Motion for order requiring Tom to produce documents.

October 8 comes and goes. Tom does not produce any more documents. In anticipation of Tom's not producing the documents, Agent 657 engages counsel from FRO to prepare the motion record for a court hearing before the Associate Judge on October 8. On the close of November 7, Agent 657 serves Macy Schwabas and files with the court a copy of the motion record.

In the motion record, Agent 657 recites the history of the case since the support order was made more than 3 years ago, and the efforts of Jones,

Wilson, former lawyers, to examine Tom Richardson with two certificates of non-attendance and excuses about his records being destroyed in a warehouse flood.

A couple of days before the hearing, Macy Schwabas serves a reply affidavit of Tom Richardson explaining the delays, namely not having a lawyer available at the time of the examination, the TTC subway breakdown on the second occasion, and a copy of the Small Claims Court statement of claim against Aero Warehousing for damages up to $35,000 for loss of records.

Hearing before Associate Judge Dobbs.

"Your Honour, my name is Joanne Stacy. I am representing FRO. My colleague is Macy Schwabas. He represents Tom Richardson. With the court's permission, I have Mr. Stanley Mah sitting beside me. He has had carriage of the enforcement file on behalf of Beth Richardson at FRO. Ms. Richardson is sitting at the back of the courtroom on the left side."

After reviewing the facts and the details of the support order, they present their argument. Associate Judge Dobbs grants the order directing Tom Richardson to produce the documents set out in the notice of examination within 60 days, but Associate Judge Dobbs advises that his reasons to do so will be released in 2 weeks.

Associate Judge Dobbs is experienced having served on the bench as a Master for 15 years. He needs the time to express his reasons and needs time to research why he has ordered Tom Richardson to produce documents.

Tom Richardson immediately appeals the ruling to the Superior Court of Justice even though he does not have the reasons for ordering him to produce the documents.

Another 3 months pass before the hearing can be set down. Associate Judge Dobbs releases his reasons after which time, Macy Schwabas schedules the appeal. The reasons outline the history of the case and Tom Richardson's attempt to delay and frustrate Beth Richardson's right to collect on the support order.

To short-circuit the proceedings and avoid more hearings, the FRO also applies for an order that Tom Richardson be held in contempt. If Tom Richardson's appeal fails and the FRO's motion for contempt is successful, the court may imprison Tom for contempt, may punish Tom by fine or imprisonment, or by both, for a fine up to $10,000 and imprisonment not exceeding 180 days.

Despite being debtor-friendly, Ontario has strict enforcement proceedings for persons who abuse the law and orders made by courts. If the person purges his or her contempt, the court will likely forgive the person with a severe warning. Tom's case borders that fine line between one who appears to comply with the law and one who frustrates any attempt to follow the law.

Macy meets with Tom at Macy's office early in November. Macy reads the 'Riot Act' to Tom, bluntly saying if the FRO are successful, Tom is likely to go to jail. Tom got the message.

Tom produces full copies of his tax returns, title documents to the house, income, and expense statements for the last 12 months, insurance policies, and an affidavit from the president of Aero Warehousing. The affidavit attests that Tom and the company's files were destroyed in a water flood on the premises caused by a leaky sprinkler system that was running for several days. Tom had to settle the case with Aero Warehousing in exchange for that affidavit.

Macy calls Agent 657 and offers the documents and affidavit. Macy scans the documents and forwards them to Agent 657. On December 1, Agent 657 calls Macy Schwabas to tell him that FRO will not be taking a position on the appeal and adjourns its motion for a contempt order on the condition that Tom Richardson agrees to attend an examination within 20 days. The appeal is set for January 10.

On the morning of January 9, Macy Schwabus advises Agent 657 that Tom Richardson agrees to the terms of the order, and March 3 is set for the next examination.

March 3, Next Examination

Back to the examination on March 3. "Are you ready, Mr. Richardson?" says Agent 657.

"Mr. Richardson, your lawyer Mr. Schwabas has produced full copies of your tax returns for the years 2012 to 2016. Please look at them and advise if they are yours."

Tom pauses. He looks at each document, one by one, and then, "Yes, they are."

"I am going to make your tax returns for the years 2012 and 2016 exhibit no. 1."

"Mr. Schwabas, do you have any objections?"

"No."

Agent 657 uses the stamp on the desk and presses it on a blank sheet of paper attached to the tax returns. He completes the stamp by marking the name of the case and inserts the date.

"Mr. Richardson, your lawyer Mr. Schwabas has produced copies of income and expense statements for the last 12 months. Please look at them and advise if they are yours."

Again, Tom takes his time to look at each income and expense statement. He looks at each statement, one by one, and says, "Yes, they are."

"I am going to make your income and expense statements for the last 12 months exhibit no. 2."

"Mr. Schwabas, do you have any objections?"

"No."

"Now, Mr. Richardson, starting with exhibit 1, pointing to his signature on the last page of each of the returns, is this your signature?"

"Yes."

"Are these entries correct?"

"I assume so. I didn't put them in."

"Who did?"

"I do not know. It could have been either the bookkeeper or the accountant or both."

"Where did these numbers come from?"

"I don't know."

"Mr. Richardson, if you read the sentence above your signature, you will see that you certify that the entries are true and correct. Take another look, Mr. Richardson."

"Yes, as I have already told you, these numbers were inserted by either the bookkeeper or the accountant or both. I relied on them to complete the returns."

"What about the income and expense statements? Exhibit 2. Where did these figures come from?"

"I do not know."

"At the bottom of each statement is your printed name and signature. Is that correct?"

"Yes."

"Did you prepare these statements?"

"No."

"Who did?"

"The bookkeeper or the accountant [pause] or both."

"Mr. Schwabas, we are not much further than at the conclusion of the last examination. While we have the documents, we do not have source of the numbers. Unless Mr. Richardson is going to be more cooperative, I am going back to the court."

Macy Schwabas did not react. He said nothing.

The examination stopped.

Next Motion

Agent 657 prepares another motion before Associate Judge Dobbs. One year later, four years after the initial support order, Beth is no further ahead. Another year of frustration, and no money to buy food and clothing. Beth and Rick are now living in rental accommodation with 3 months behind in rent. Beth complains to Agent 657, but Agent 657 cannot pay her bills. He can only empathize with Beth and try to move the case forward.

Agent 657 calls the court several times in an effort to get an earlier date for the motion. However, Agent 657 has to serve Betty Wight, the bookkeeper, and Chris Honest, the accountant, with the process. As of March, Agent 657 arranges a date in the second week of July, July 15, after conferring with Macy Schwabas. Macy expects the motion is for another order compelling Tom Richardson to testify, but when he receives a copy of the motion, he chuckles.

Agent 657 knew his stuff. His motion was for an order giving FRO the right to examine the bookkeeper and the accountant. Agent 657 was not able to serve Betty Wight. She had moved, and no one seemed to know where.

Ultimately, when FRO served Chris Honest with a copy of the motion, Agent 657 called him and explained that he needed to examine him on how Tom Richardson's tax returns and income and expense statements were prepared. At the same time, Agent 657 obtained the last known address for Betty Wight. Betty decided to retire after Tom was shot by his son. Not only did she retire, but she moved back to Lethbridge where her husband's family have a home.

Agent 657 proceeded to serve her with the motion and upon service in Lethbridge, he called her to suggest that she retain a lawyer if necessary. When she spoke to Agent 657, Betty had no reason not to testify.

On July 15, Joanne Stacy appeared in court on behalf of FRO and Beth Richardson and Macy Schwabas on behalf of Tom Richardson. Associate Judge Dobbs said:

"Welcome, Ms. Stacy and Mr. Schwabas. Is this the same case as I heard over a year ago?"

Ms. Stacy: "Yes, Sir. After we received your reasons, Mr. Schwabas appealed to the judge. FRO also applied for a contempt order. Fortunately, Mr. Richardson complied with your order, sir."

"What brings you here today? I read your notice of motion for an order permitting FRO the right to examine Betty Wight and Chris Honest."

"Mr. Richardson produced the documents including full tax returns and income and expense statements. However, when I attempted to examine him on the entries, he said that he did not know anything about the numbers."

"Let me look at the motion record, Ms. Stacy."

Pause for 6 minutes while Associate Judge Dobbs re-reads the material.

"Mr. Schwabas, what do you have to say?"

"I have two submissions, Your Honour. First, FRO has examined Mr. Richardson now two times. FRO has completed its examination. If you look at the last page of the second transcript, it is clear that FRO reserved its right to bring Mr. Richardson back to continue the examination.

"The questions Agent 657 asked relate to a discussion on the preparation of the tax returns and income and expense statements. On page 32, line 18 and following, Agent 657 asks questions about the numbers, but he did not ask questions about the source of the numbers. He did not ask for the back-up documents that support the numbers. Mr. Richardson gave the documents to his bookkeeper and to his accountant to prepare the returns.

"It's not for me, Your Honour, to give Agent 657 tips on questioning my client. Simply put, Agent 657 has concluded his examination, or if he has not completed it, he did not ask the right questions. In my submission, he is finished.

"I have provided Ms. Stacy and the court with two cases that say, in effect, the court should not order third parties to testify in an examination in aid of execution if the creditor has completed the examination.

"I submit that the evidence is clear that FRO has completed its examination, and therefore the motion should be dismissed.

"Second, Ms. Betty Wight is no longer in Toronto or in the province of Ontario. She has moved back to Lethbridge Alberta where her husband's family lives. I submit that the court does not have the jurisdiction to order that Betty Wight return to Ontario to testify. Those are my submissions."

"Thank you, Mr. Schwabas. Ms. Stacy, do you have any reply?"

"Yes, Your Honour. It's matter of semantics. I agree with Mr. Schwabas to some extent. The examination is completed, to a point. But it is not completed to the point where Mr. Richardson has put blocks in our way. We cannot ask any more questions without the assistance of the bookkeeper and the accountant. And to that extent, the examination is not completed."

Pause.

"I am going to make the order, Ms. Stacy. However, I agree with Mr. Schwabas that this court cannot compel Ms. Wight to return to Ontario. I am prepared to order her to testify if and when she does return to Ontario. And I make the order directing Mr. Chris Honest to attend for examination. Thank you both."

Chapter Nine
Motion to Vary Initial Order

Tom applied to the court to vary the amount of spousal support in response to Beth's motion to hold Tom in contempt of court for breaching various orders. Tom sought to extinguish the spousal support arrears, now totaling some $250,000 and to reduce his monthly spousal support payments in the future.

He claimed that he has not been able to work and effectively he is insolvent. Macy Schwabus threw a curve. His motion to vary the support order had to be brought in the original divorce action. FRO was the enforcement arm of the support order. Unfortunately, FRO could not argue that motion; it had to be argued by the original lawyer, Heidi Mattews.

Several years ago, the court awarded Beth support payments of $5,000 monthly. At that time, the court thought that Tom's income was substantially more, and rather than expanding the trial proceedings, the court imputed income to Tom despite his counsel's opposition.

Tom appealed, but before the appeal was heard, Beth brought a motion to require him to pay security for costs as he had paid very little on the support order, and the court so ordered that Tom pay $27,500 into court as security for costs if he was unsuccessful on the appeal.

Tom unsuccessfully appealed that support order in 2015 suggesting that imputing income was a guessing game without factual information to predict income. However, the appeal court was sympathetic to the motion court judge as she had little information on which to base her decision.

If Tom wanted to supply more current and accurate information, the appeal court said it would take another look and refer the issue back to the motion court judge to achieve a fair result. Tom did nothing. After several years, Tom has paid approximately $15,250.00 and was now in substantial arrears.

Tom now argues before a different judge that his life and circumstances have changed over the last 4 years for the worse. He longer works as an employee, but works part-time as a self-employed photographer for a small number of advertising agencies in Canada and overseas in Western Europe that focus on new styles in women's clothing.

Tom argues that his numbers are nowhere near what he was making in 2015. Tom produces, through his lawyer Macy Schwabus, his tax returns over the last 4 years showing a significant decline in gross income from $225,000 to just over $40,000 in the last year.

The court was now faced with dismissing Tom's motion to vary the support payments or setting new numbers based on his present income numbers.

Tom appears with his first family law lawyer, Tim Harrigan. They enter the Court House on University Avenue passing through security and onto the escalator and proceed to the second floor.

On the wall adjacent to the escalator is a list of all the court cases for the day and their respective courtroom numbers. Richardson v. Richardson, their case, is assigned to motion courtroom B3. The courtroom is a smaller courtroom usually reserved for motions brought by lawyers without any person giving evidence or taking the stand. Two hours have been marked for the hearing.

"My name, Your Honour, is Tim Harrigan, appearing for Thomas Richardson. My colleague, Ms. Matthews, appears for Beth Richardson."

"I have your motion record Mr. Harrigan, and yours as well Ms. Matthews. How do you wish to proceed, Mr. Harrigan," said Judge Armstrong.

"Well, Your Honour, I would like to call Mr. Richardson to the stand and give his evidence. He has had a difficult 4 years coping with the shooting by his son, his wife's attempt to run or ruin his business and he is now facing bankruptcy. I also have two subpoenas that are being served on Mr. Richardson's accountant and medical practitioner. They will testify about Mr. Richardson's financial woes and his ill health."

"This is motions court," said Judge Armstrong. "You know that, Mr. Harrigan. We don't hear parties or witnesses. Besides, his affidavit is complete. I have read it. So, what more can he add?"

"I suggest we adjourn this proceeding to a date to be arranged and fixed for live witnesses. We will need a whole day, from 10 in the morning to 4:30 in the afternoon to hear this. We will need a court reporter. Alternatively, I can have the accountant and medical practitioner prepare affidavits and then allow Ms. Matthews to cross-examine them if she so wishes."

Beth nudges Ms. Matthews. "No, we can't have another adjournment. It's going on all too long."

"Your Honour, may I speak?" said Ms. Matthews.

"This is the third time that this motion has been scheduled to be heard. The two previous hearings stretch back to 7 months. Nothing happened. The motion records have been filed. There have been no cross-examinations. We are ready to proceed today."

"Well, Mr. Harrigan. What do you have to say?"

"The accountant's evidence is critical to the motion. His evidence will show that my client is in financial distress and need of relief. The medical doctor's evidence will show that my client is not physically able to work any harder than he has over the last 4 years. Without their evidence, I might as well withdraw the motion."

The judge was caught between two poles, denying Mr. Richardson's state of financial health and personal health versus another delay to Mrs. Richardson who has not collected her support payments.

The judge had read the materials and was ready to proceed. The judge needed to hear from counsel before the day's end.

Judge Armstrong whispers to his registrar. Call the administration booking office to see what is available over the next 30 days. Minutes later, the registrar advises the judge that nothing is available for 6 months. All judges and courtrooms are booked. Subject to cancelations and postponements, nothing was available.

Reluctantly, the judge adjourns the case to a special hearing on an expedited basis. The judge instructs Mr. Harrigan to serve his affidavits within 21 days and directs Ms. Matthews to cross-examine the deponents if she so chooses within the following 14 days. In the meantime, the registrar has to find a full day to hear this matter.

Special Hearing Day

Four months later, the registrar of the court notifies both lawyers by email of the special hearing day.

This was a special day for both Tom and Beth. They were already into the fifth year without any resolution of the major issues. Tom wanted to vary the initial support order from an award of $5,000 down to $2,000 when he could afford it.

In addition, Tom wanted an order varying the support order retroactively. In other words, Tom wanted the court to retroactively wipe out all the arrears, or in any event, reduce the arrears down to an amount that he could handle. This was a high onus. Tom had to show sufficient material changes once the initial order was made. Tom had to show where, under his present circumstances, that to continue with the support order arrears would be unfair, if not unjust.

Tom wanted an order going forward that he should pay $2,000 a month. Like the arrears, Tom had to show material and substantial changes to his income before the court will consider varying the support order. Were the circumstances significant or substantial? How long did they last? Were the circumstances foisted on him or did he create the circumstances?

On the other hand, Beth too had been prejudiced. She had been a dutiful and loving wife until the parties separated. She had a better-than-middle-class lifestyle with a suburban home and raised two children as a part-time homemaker. She was receiving $9,000 monthly until the business collapsed, and now after four years, could not even receive the $5,000 a month that the court endorsed. Tom was in substantial arrears. Beth was living on the gifts from her parents.

Tom took the stand. He testified, and the court found:

- Tom was previously employed by his company; the company is controlled by a trust directed by Tom's friend.
- Tom is now self-employed.
- Tom has failed to provide financial statements over the last 5 years.
- Tom spends several months a year in Europe.
- Tom diverted income from himself to Wendy. Tom did not mention this in his affidavit nor in his oral testimony.
- Tom did not produce documents showing the disposition of his expenses including food and clothing.
- Tom did not include foreign income on his tax returns.
- Tom has organized his business affairs in such a way so as to avoid his payment obligations.
- Chris Honest took the stand.

He testified and the court found:

- Chris has been Tom's accountant for many years.
- Chris did not audit Tom's business accounts;
- Chris relied on numbers given by the bookkeeper.
- Chris never saw the documents.
- The bookkeeper was not available to testify.
- The numbers on the financial statements were inconclusive.
- Beth took the stand.
- She testified, and the court found:
- She had received $9,000 monthly for many years until the business collapsed.
- Beth had a support order requiring Tom to pay $5,000 monthly.
- Beth had received only about $15,250 over 4 years when he owed over $250,000 plus costs;
- Tom was in substantial arrears.
- Beth was living on the gifts from her parents.

The court was caught. The court was faced with a dilemma. It did not have the evidence to say whether $5,000 was too much or too little. The court did not have the evidence to say that $2,000 was the right amount for support payments.

The court recessed until 2:30 in the afternoon. Heidi and Beth leave the courtroom and head down the escalator to the cafeteria. Each picked up a sandwich and a coffee and sat down at a corner table.

Heidi begins talking. She sees that Beth is visibly upset.

"Beth, the judge has to balance Tom's interest and yours. While the judge may empathize with your position, the judge cannot come down hard on Tom if he doesn't have the money.

"In these cases, the judge has a wide discretion to vary a support order going forward and a wide discretion to vary the support order retroactively. The judge has to ensure that there is a fair result having regard to Tom's income and assets."

"But what if he is hiding his income? I know he is."

"That's our job. We have to prove that he has hidden income and assets. Tom has an obligation to disclose all his income and assets so that the court can make a fair assessment."

"He's lying. How can he live so well on $30,000 to $50,000 a year? It's impossible. He must have friends who are helping him," says Beth.

"The court expects that Tom will make a full and frank disclosure of his income and assets. If he does not disclose such information, the court can assume that he is a non-cooperative support payor. You will recall Beth on the initial support order, the court imputed an income to Tom upon which the court awarded you $5,000 a month.

"Well, this is same. If the court has sufficient information and documents to support the information, the court can impute a higher amount. Right now, we don't have that evidence. Tom is even asking the judge to vary the initial order retroactively. This is unheard of."

"So, we're stuck," says Beth. "I can expect that the judge will not increase the monthly payments."

Heidi nods her head up and down. "I think so," says Heidi.

"We can expect the judge to rule against you on this point."

"What about Tom's motion to vary the arrears retroactively?"

"We have the same problem. According to Tom's tax returns over the last 4 years, his income has dropped substantially every year. The year before you split with Tom, he was earning $240,000 a year. Now, he is making between $30,000 and $40,000. On simple arithmetic, he could not pay $5,000 monthly. He is in effect bankrupt."

"You're telling me that the court could wipe out the full $250,000. That's impossible. His tax returns are false. They have to be. He is living too well on his reduced income. He must be getting the money from somewhere."

"Are you telling me that my support order, now totaling over $250,000 is in jeopardy?"

"Yes."

"All of it?"

"Yes, but not likely. That would be an extreme."

"I'm screwed," says Beth.

"I'm going to lose my arrears and now going forward; my support order is going to decrease to something less than $5,000. And you're telling me that's justice. Something is wrong with this system. I have lost faith in the judicial system. Tom's using the system to beat off my claims. That's not right. Help me, Heidi."

Following the lunch break, the parties and lawyers reconvene. The judge had thought about the case over the lunch hour.

So, the court dismissed the applications: one to increase the support order and enforce the support payments and the other to vary the previous support order.

The result was a bottom-line stand-off, a stalemate. Four years earlier, Beth had a monthly support order of $5,000 which she could not enforce. Where does she go from here? Private enforcement, then publicly funded enforcement, both proved inadequate.

Chapter Ten
Contempt Proceedings

Motion to Vary Initial Order

Beth has several orders requiring Tom to pay support. On separation, Beth was able to obtain an initial order that Tom pays her $1,250 a week or $5,000 monthly commencing immediately and payable monthly. Tom appealed, and then at the eleventh hour, abandoned the appeal.

Tom failed to pay Beth from the outset. Beth returned to the court for an order compelling him to pay the arrears with a proviso that if he failed to pay the support payments, Beth could return to the court to have the order enforced through contempt proceedings.

Beth also obtained an order requiring him to pay costs of the proceedings in the amount of $34,000 plus disbursements to date. Tom appeared with his lawyer, Macy Schwabus, at each court hearing. Tom was clearly aware of the support orders and the possibility that he could be held in contempt.

Tom, however, keeps ignoring these orders. Ultimately, after consultation with her friends and lawyer, Ms. Stacy from FRO and Beth decide to bring contempt proceedings against Tom. If granted, the court has the power to fine Tom and to imprison him for his abuse in flaunting an order of the court.

Courts in Ontario are reluctant to imprison support payors for breach of support orders. However, given the right case, the circumstances of the abuse, and the right judge, the court will find the support payor in contempt. The penalty for contempt in family law matters is usually a fine and imprisonment. How long?

That's a matter to discuss. It could vary from a few days over the weekend to 60 days to 180 days. However, imprisonment was not the way to go. Imprisonment would only enflame the situation. It would take Tom out of the working force and make him antagonistic toward Beth. Imprisonment was not the answer.

Once Beth brought the motion, Tom countered again, the second time, with a motion to vary the support payments and retroactively wipe the slate clean of any obligation. Beth argued that her motion be held first. Tom, however, said if he were successful in varying the support order, the need for a hearing on whether he was in contempt was moot or meaningless. The court agreed with Tom.

Tom's defence to the contempt proceedings was his inability to comply with the order; or in other words, he did not have the money to pay the support payments. On the other hand, Beth's counsel, Ms. Stacy, would argue that Tom created the situation where he was unable to pay the support. Therefore, his defence should not apply.

Once again, the court was faced with a dilemma: whether to imprison Tom for failure to obey the court orders or excuse him from making payments as he did not have the income to pay.

Beth was in disbelief. Sitting at the back with her friend Joyce and son, Ricky, she could not believe the discussion between her counsel, Tom's counsel, and the judge. She thought that this is not a case where Tom doesn't have the money. She knew he did have the money but had secreted his assets away to avoid execution. He was feigning poverty; he was doctoring his tax returns; he was hiding his income flow. How could she prove it?

After going back and forth with argument, the judge decided to adjourn the motion for contempt to another day pending a case conference in chambers with another judge where the clients can speak freely.

Beth was noticeably upset. Another adjournment, another day, another judge. When will this nightmare be over? Beth was losing faith in the judicial system. Her issues were not getting resolved. But maybe she was asking for too much. If Tom didn't have the money, she could probably understand. She would not like the situation, but could reluctantly accept it. On the other hand, she 'knew' Tom was not suffering. She "knew" he was living well with his new friend.

Chapter Eleven
Parliament

A Long Night

Weeks after the motion to commit Tom for failure to pay support, Beth stands in front of her bathroom sink and starts to sob. It's around midnight. Rick is fast asleep on the living room sofa. She pauses, looking at the mirror on the cabinet door. She opens the door and stares at the bottle of sleeping pills.

Without hesitation, she opens the bottle and proceeds to swallow all the pills washing them down with several cups full of water. She then walks over to her bed, lies down, and stares at the ceiling.

Beth overdoes in her bedroom before going to sleep in her one-bedroom apartment. She overdoses on pills taken to relieve her anxiety, pain, and stress.

When Rick woke the following morning, he went to see his mother only to find that she was lifeless. Calling 911, Rick waited impatiently for the ambulance to arrive minutes later. Rick was visibly shaken. His tears kept running down his face, then drying up, and then start coming again. Rick had the front double doors wide open so that the paramedics could easily carry her out on a stretcher. Rushing in, two paramedics quickly took her pulse, lifted her onto a gurney, and rushed her into a waiting elevator.

Rick kept pressing the paramedics for a readout, but they said nothing.

"Is she OK? Tell me, is she OK?" tears rolling down Rick's face.

They said nothing.

"Where are you taking her? Which hospital?"

"We don't know yet. Once we are in the ambulance, the dispatcher will tell us where we are going."

"Can I ride with you?"

"Come on, this is urgent," said one of the paramedics.

Parliament Debates

2:15 PM

While Parliament is sitting, there is question and answer period in the House of Commons each day for about 45 minutes to allow Members of Parliament to question the government about news items, policy decisions, announcements, and legislation. This feature has been a tradition since 1967 when Parliament was established in Canada.

On this day, there is a vigorous debate on increasing the salaries of the Members of Parliament and increasing their pensions. The House debates over increasing the salaries of the Members of Parliament by 3% and increasing their pensions by 2% per year.

Many Members speak out in favour of the increases; while some Members speak out against the increases.

To those who approve the increases, Members state that there has not been any increase in salary and in pensions for over 5 years. It's time to pay our Members of Parliament a fair wage so that we can attract better candidates to represent the people of our nation. Without such increases, we will stagnate and leave the government to operate without qualified help.

"If we are going to pay them low wages, we cannot attract better people," says the Honourable Member from Peterborough. "We must remain competitive."

"Competitive, yes. Don't you think we are now paid too much," says the Honourable Member from Fundy Royal. From the public's perception. "We are overpaid and underworked. We have too many people employed in the federal government. We need to do more work as Members of Parliament instead of creating mini-fiefdoms of workers. It's time we earn our keep in this House."

The Members of Parliament continue to argue about the size of their pension plan. Yelling, screaming, oblivious to the social issues around themselves, John Matthews, MP, points to the Speaker of House and yells, "I would like to address Parliament on an urgent issue facing family breakups."

He makes several attempts to get the Speaker's attention.

He yells, "Point of order, point of order."

"I want to address Parliament today. I want to address the House today about one of my constituents," but few are listening.

Banging the desk to get the Members' attention and yelling at the Speaker, to get his attention, and finally, after many more seconds, the Speaker acknowledges his right.

The Speaker, "Quiet please, quiet please."

John Matthews stands up.

Mr. Mathews stands up and addresses the Speaker and the Members.

"Mr. Prime Minister, the Honourable Speaker of the House, fellow colleagues, and staff members, I rise not to support raising salaries or pensions to our members nor to support keeping the status quo and encouraging the government to become more accountable.

"I rise because this debate is self-centred and ignores the true state of affairs of our working public sector. We have 13% unemployment rate in Canada; we have 400,000 immigrants yearly and we still cannot afford to protect our indigenous and give them clean water. Perhaps if we each gave 1% of our salary to fund a clean water program, we would receive less criticism from the opposition and from the media.

"I stand here today to tell you about an unfortunate situation.

"Mr. Speaker, I would like to make a presentation about a very serious problem facing our country. I would appreciate if this House would listen rather than bicker about receiving more pensions when members retire. When we as a country opened up the doors to our divorce laws in the early 1970s, we failed to enlist the provinces and territories with respect to spousal and child support.

"Our divorce and family laws are a disgrace today. While they may have been successful in the 1970s, they no longer protect the support creditor and the children of the marriage. In most cases, the support creditor is the woman. Most are left without support in raising children.

"Consequently, most spousal support creditors are forced into the welfare system of our 3 levels of government. With the lack of coordinated services, spousal support creditors are forced into submission. They cannot fight the support debtor in court; they cannot fight the support debtor in the media; they cannot maintain the basic needs of life. In short, the justice system has failed them. We have failed them.

"One such spousal support creditor, a constituent of Toronto Spadina, lies in a Toronto hospital since last week in a coma. Her name is Beth Richardson.

"Eight years ago, my constituent was married to a successful businessman in the advertising sector with 2 grown-up children. Once a happily married woman, she became disillusioned with her life in her mid-40s. My constituent and her husband began parting their ways in early 2013.

"With grown-up children, there was an empty nest. They found that they had less in common than in the first 20 years of their marriage. As they began to part company and go their separate ways, the marriage quickly disintegrated into 'he said, she said' arguments. Ultimately, she went one way and he another.

"After a trial period of separation of 6 months, she and her husband decided to divorce. Initially, her husband Tom agreed to support her and their two grown-up children in a lifestyle of their marriage. But then Tom reneged on his promise, and after 8 ½ years in the Ontario Superior Court of Justice in Toronto, then another year in the Ontario Court of Appeal, and lastly yet another year in Tom's failed attempt to get leave of the Supreme Court of Canada, the game was over.

"Beth was broke. After 8 ½ years into our judicial system, she couldn't pay her lawyers, some of whom acted for her pro bono. Beth tried every technique possible to gain payment. She used the legal system to the fullest. She went to Pro Bono and Justice Net in Toronto, but after a few unsuccessful hearings, they gave up. Then she went to FRO, the Family Responsibility Office in Ontario which assists people like Beth to collect support. But all these systems failed her.

"Then, she used the family connection guilt, but that too failed. She used her children, mature young adults to assist. But one child sided with her, and the other broke family ties. Beth Richardson was obsessed. She was despondent. She was depressed. She attempted suicide and is now awakening from a coma in a Toronto hospital. She is fighting for her own life in despair and in submission to an archaic system.

"So where are our family laws today? Have they improved since the 1970s? Do we need more suicides and attempted suicides before this House recognizes that family law no longer protects the parties. It's time for us to protect the family unit.

"For 8 1/2 years, they fought in court. Initially, she was entitled to $5,000 monthly support. That took 2 years of court attendance. In attempting to collect on the $5,000 monthly, the divorce stalled. It took 31 court appearances in total from 2013 to 2019 before 8 different judges to enforce the support order. Of these 31 court appearances, 3 were appeals to the Ontario Court of Appeal, and 2 hearings attempting to enforce 2 contempt orders. The case would still be going on but for her submission to the judicial system.

"Those of you who are lawyers or have had legal training know our family law courts are backlogged. Everyone here knows of a person who has gone through the family law courts with disdain. We spend our time here arguing over increases in salary and pension when the very fact of society is based on fair representation and access to justice. We have failed miserably Mr. Speaker.

"Beth Richardson, a beautiful woman lost confidence in our justice system after many years of attempting to collect support from her ex-not-so-dead-beat partner. Our debate today over raises in pay and in pension pales in comparison to the hundreds of thousands of support creditors who cannot recover payments through the justice system.

"Family matters have tied up our courts for decades at tremendous expense to the parties involved and at the public expense of maintaining a large component of family law judges. There has been no substantial reform for decades:

- We have not coordinated our legislation with the provinces and the territories.
- We have not updated the Divorce Act.
- We have not provided adequate enforcement procedures to allow support creditors to collect their payments.
- We have not leveled the playing field in 50 years.
- We have not kept pace with our growing society.

"Mr. Prime Minister, the Honourable Speaker of the House, fellow Members, I urge you to rethink you're raising the wages and pensions today and to begin focusing on the lives of your constituents and their daily trials. Many have submitted with total frustration to archaic attempts to protect support creditors. Many have died in vain having submitted to a judicial system that is insensitive and out of touch with our society.

"Thank you for listening. As you can hear me, and see me with tears in my eyes, I urge you to rethink about why you are here today."

"Here, here," roared the Members of Parliament.

"Mr. Speaker of the House, may I address the House?" said the Prime Minister.

"Yes, by all means," said the Speaker.

"Fellow colleagues, Members of Parliament from whatever party or affiliation, Mr. Mathews, I strongly endorse an immediate Committee review of family law legislation not only on a federal level but also in coordination with the provinces and territories. It is my desire that something good should come from this constituent who submitted to a failed judicial system."

Chapter Twelve
Revival

More years pass. No new legislation is in sight. Family law justice just doesn't have the political will.

So where are our family laws today? Have they improved since the 1970s? Do we need more suicides, assaults, and battered women before this House recognizes that family law and relationships are broken? It's time to protect the family.

Beth recovered from a near-suicide-attempt. Weekly, she was seeing a stress counselor and also a therapist sponsored by the hospital. Both were teaching Beth to cope with the reality that she was not going to collect support from Tom. Beth had a reality check.

She was broke. It's been a terrible 8 ½ years for her. After 8 ½ years into our judicial system, she couldn't pay her lawyers, some of whom acted for her pro bono. Beth tried every technique possible to gain payment. She used the legal system to the fullest. But it failed her. She used the family connection guilt, but that too failed. She used her children, mature young adults to assist. But one child sided with her, and the other broke family ties. Beth Richardson was obsessed. She was despondent. She was in depression for years.

"Beth, are you there?"

Her old friend Joyce was on the line.

"Let's have lunch. I have a new idea."

"Joyce, thank you but I need a break. I have had enough of lawyers and judges and court protocol. I have had enough of being told what to wear, when to talk and what to say, and then how to say it with emotion. Enough. I have an order more than 8 years ago and I can't get paid.

"What kind of judicial system do we have? I want to give up and live out my life with gifts from my parents and from you. You have been really kind to me. My parents are in their senior-senior years and need the money for caregivers. Enough. I have had enough."

"Stop it. Shut up. It's not over yet. I have a new idea. I'll meet you at Trattoria's for lunch today at noon. I'll make the reservation under my name. Be there."

Joyce hangs up.

Beth, still in her nightdress, debates with herself whether to get dressed or call her therapist for help. Beth flips a coin: heads call the therapist; tales go to lunch. Beth throws the coin into the air, and it lands tales up. Beth is going for lunch.

Beth cleans up, puts on some facial make-up, and gets into a summer dress that compliments her aging beauty. There's no doubt that she stands out as a beautiful woman in her early 50s.

They meet at Trattoria's. They sit out-doors on the patio. Joyce arrives first, and orders 2 martinis, straight up with a twist and olives. Minutes later, Beth arrives at the same time as the martinis. Beth goes over to Joyce, gives her a kiss on each cheek, and then sits down.

"Here's to you, Beth. I've got another idea to beat Tom. Are you ready?"

"Let's drink first and then order. I'm going to need some food and drink in me first before you tell me about a new idea."

Joyce summons the waitress. The waitress comes over.

"Can I help you?"

"Yes, we will have 2 chicken Caesar salads. Thank you."

Joyce leans over the table sipping her martini. "I have a young lawyer who might take your case. Well, he is in his 40s, probably in late 40s. He with a small law firm in North York. He comes from a relatively comfortable family. Really, he does not have to work for a living. But he likes difficult cases because most litigators will shy away from such cases as they tend to be too costly without any guarantee of results.

"As you know, these cases, much like yours, go on for years without any resolution. I met him at the golf club, and he impressed me with some knowledge of your case. As I understand, some cases get reported, and if so, the Law Society records them in reports for the profession. Anyway, he read one or two of the reports and was familiar with the general facts; namely, that you got an award, but couldn't collect. That's it. Do you want to meet him?"

Beth didn't say anything. She had been courteous to Joyce as a long-time friend and confidant. But now Joyce had taken the next step. Joyce didn't want to give up on her friend, in need.

"Let me think about it," said Beth.

"No, there's nothing to think about. It's a free meeting, and if he takes your case, it's still free. Eventually, someone will listen. All you need is ONE judge to say 'that's it. Pay or else.'"

Beth was at her end. Eight and a half years of fighting with no real results sound like such a waste of time and money, leaving aside the emotional toll. With support debts totaling over $500,000, she might as well put Tom into bankruptcy. Even then, the debt may get wiped out when he gets his discharge.

Beth said, "OK, set it up." And Beth set it up.

No sooner than Beth says OK, Joyce picks up her cell phone, calls Eli Jordan. "Hi, it's me. Can you come over?"

Eli was sitting at another table inside the restaurant. Seconds later, he walked over to Joyce's table and introduced himself to Beth.

"Hello, my name is Eli Jordan. You are Beth Richardson. May I sit down?"

Beth was shocked. Not in a negative way, but one thankful for Joyce is setting up this interview.

Eli summoned the waitress again. "Make it 3 chicken Caesars and one more vodka martini. Thank you."

All three chatted amicably with Beth wiping away tears as she recalled several of the steps that had been taken over the years, with some positive results, but overall with disdain of the system. There were flashbacks to Heidi Mattews, Arnold Jones, Tim Harrigan, and of course, Macy Schwabus.

Eli did not know any of these lawyers, but he had heard of Macy Schwabus who was known for his skill and techniques in defending debtors.

"I would like to help," said Eli.

"I would like to try something new. Courts in Ontario and elsewhere have yet to recognize orders made against third parties who assist the debtor in camouflaging or hiding assets or just giving benefits to the debtor that they would otherwise receive but for the judgment or order."

"I don't understand."

"Well, here we have a debtor, your ex-husband Tom. He says he has no assets, no income to pay your support order. Yet, he lives as though he has the money. He lives in a penthouse apartment in downtown Toronto; he drives a relatively new BMW; he travels to Europe on a regular basis with his new friend. He eats out frequently. He entertains his new girlfriend.”

“Where did you get all this information?”

“One or two judgments ago, the court summarized much of the proceedings but did not proceed to hold Tom in contempt. Some of the cases are reported for public access.

“So, someone is paying the rent on his penthouse apartment; someone is making the lease payments on his BMW and someone has expenditures for airline tickets on his or her credit card and expenses for his trips to Europe. I want to make that someone pay an equivalent amount of these benefits to you!”

“Good luck!” says Beth.

“No, I need a judge who will do it. That’s my job.”

“What’s in it for you?”

“The challenge. You have been hurt by the judicial system, by outdated family law legislation. I may charge you a fee down the road, but only if you have the money to pay. Otherwise, I will try to get my fees from that someone, perhaps from Tom, too.

“I am empathetic to your case. I want the courts to try to rectify the situation as it seems Parliament needs another 100 years to go by before this topic strikes their interest. We need a whole new generation that put the people first before the politicians. I hope that’s my grandchildren’s generation that wakes up Parliament.”

After finishing their salads and martinis, Joyce picks up the bill. Beth stands up, leans over to kiss Joyce, and sticks out her hand to Eli.

“Thank you for your time and interest. Do you have a card?”

Eli gives her his professional card.

“Thank you again.” Beth leaves.

Chapter Thirteen
Retribution

Joyce prods Beth into retaining Eli Jordan.

"Give it one last try. Your case and thousands like you out there deserve better and fairer treatment in the courts. It's a story worth telling. I have confidence in Eli's exposing the hole in the system. All you need is one judge, just one judge, to open the door."

Beth and Rick attend Eli Jordan's office on north Yonge Street at 2 in the afternoon. She brings all the copies of the pleadings and final briefs. Parking underneath the office tower, she needs help as they are in banker's boxes stored in her trunk. Rick has a make-shift trolley. He unloads the trunk and places 3 boxes on the trolley and proceeds with Beth to the elevator. Eli Jordan has an office on the 10th floor facing south overlooking downtown Toronto's skyscrapers.

Beth calls ahead so Eli will meet them as the elevator opens. He escorts them into the board room.

"Please, sit down. Can I get you a soft drink, perhaps some tea? I'm having some myself."

Beth and Rick decline. Eli helps himself to a cup. Pours hot water over the tea bag.

"Let me make you a cup of tea," looking at Beth.

Reluctantly, Beth accepts.

Fortunately, Beth was meticulous. She recorded every motion, pleading, and order. She handed Eli a chronological list of pleadings. Motion after motion; supporting affidavits; orders, appeal notices, appeal books, judgments, reasons, etc.

"Well, I've got lots to read. You made my life easier with the index. Thank you."

Eli takes a copy from the copy machine in the board room.

"Let's go over the timetable. Beth, can you briefly lead me through the steps?"

Beth briefly goes over the chronology, one date after another. Eli takes copious notes. One document at a time. Eli stops her now and then and asks questions. This takes 1 ½ hours before they are finished. Each motion brought more tears to Beth's eyes. She was re-living the motions, the court hearings, and then the appeals. Apart from the initial support order, all the motions and examinations seemed futile.

Rick pipes up.

"What are you going to do for my mom?"

"I am going to argue that your father lives too well on the money he has declared. I am going to ask the judge to make an order effectively putting your father under the financial guardianship of a receiver until all the arrears of support orders have been paid and arrangements are made for future payments."

"What's that? Is there precedent for this? Is this something new?"

"No, there is no precedent for this. Yes, it is something new."

"Can you explain this a little more?" says Rick.

"I am going to ask the judge to make an order that your father accounts to a receiver for all his expenses and activities on a monthly basis. A receiver is usually a chartered professional accountant who has some experience in monitoring businesses that are in financial difficulties."

"How can my mother pay you?"

"She can't. I am not asking her for any money, except $1.00 as a retainer. If I am successful, I will ask the judge to order your father pay my fees and expenses. OK?"

"Yeah, that's great Mr. Jordan. My father broke up this marriage and hustled my girlfriend. That's unforgivable. Make him pay."

"I am going to need a few weeks to read all this material. I know that I will have some questions for you when I am finished. We should schedule an appointment for at least 2 hours sometime during the month of June. Let me take a look at my diary. How about June 17 at 2 PM?"

"It sounds alright today. If there is a problem, I will let you know."

****

Eli did his homework

Eli did his homework. Six months later and more examinations, Eli had covered all his bases. He examined Melissa; he interviewed the bookkeeper in Lethbridge; he examined the accountant, Chris Honest; he examined the executors of the Tom Richardson Trust I and II; and finally, he examined Andrew Hall.

The court hearing came on. Macy Schwabus continued to represent Tom, but this time, Beth's new lawyer, Eli Jordan, had done a great job painting Tom to be scoundrel using the justice system to Beth's detriment. This time around, Eli Jordan had joined Heather Marshall, Melissa Rothbart, and Andrew Hall as third parties to the motion.

Macy was an experienced creditor-debtor lawyer. He knew the case law. He knew the boundaries of justice. While the onus was on Beth to prove her case, Macy knew that one day a judge may lower the boom.

Macy recommended that Tom make a deal with Beth, but Tom was insistent that the judge would follow old law and not appoint a receiver. It was more than a flip of the coin, weighted in Tom's favour. Tom was gambling that the court would not set a new precedent of appointing a third person to monitor his expenses. Even if it did, there was always an appeal.

Court Hearing

In Eli Jordan's motion record of some 4250 pages, Eli set out in great detail and with a chronology of all the hearings to paint a picture of wealth without money. How could this be?

He set out:

- The initial support order;
- The subsequent appeals;
- The subsequent withdrawal of the appeal;
- Each examination in aid of execution;
- The motions to compel Tom to attend the examinations, and affidavits in support;
- The motions to compel him to produce the documents including tax returns, and the affidavits in support;
- The motions for contempt, and the affidavits in support;
- The appeals;

- Leave to appeal;
- The transcripts of Tom's examinations;
- The transcript of Manny Eras;
- The transcript of Christopher Honest;
- The transcript of Andy Hall's examination;
- The transcript of Melissa Rothbart's examination;
- The transcript of Heather Marshall's examination;
- The certificates of non-attendance;
- The costs of maintaining the penthouse on an annual basis;
- The costs associated with Tom's overseas activities;
- The VISA card statement held in Melissa's name for the last 5 years and its analysis;
- The Mastercard statements held in Andy Hall's name for the last 5 years and its analysis; and
- The American Express statements held in Andy Hall's name for the last 5 years and its analysis.
- He painted a picture that Tom was abusing the judicial system in every possible way.
- The adjournments on the motions;
- The adjournments on the examinations;
- Booking court time knowing that the case would not get heard;
- Appealing each order; and then again;
- The fact that he never examined Mrs. Richardson on any of her affidavits.
- He painted a picture that he used the court system to invoke a balance of rights that were not in balance at all.
- He failed to disclose all his tax returns;
- He failed to disclose his credit card statements;
- He failed to disclose his health records;
- He failed to disclose the financial dive of his company.
- He painted a picture that Tom's lifestyle was beyond imagination for $30,000 to $50,000 a year.
- Tom was still driving a current BMW, owned by another;
- Tom travelled to Switzerland, France, and Italy for 3 months a year;

- Tom purchased high-end clothing several times a year on credit cards belonging to others; and
- Tom went to Blue Jay games and Raptor games.

In the end, and simply put, Beth obtained a support order of $5,000 monthly pending the divorce. Eight and half years later and no divorce, Beth has received only $15,250 with over $500,000 in arrears plus costs of $235,000. She had enlisted several lawyers to assist and finally joined the FRO to collect.

This time, the motion was different.

"Your Honour, this case cries out for help."

"Are you not overplaying this case, Mr. Jordan?"

"The facts speak for themselves. The only difference in this motion from all others is that all the evidence from over 8 years is in one place before one judge.

"I request the court's assistance to rectify a wrong committed years ago when Tom Richardson took advantage of the law to deny his wife of 24 years of marriage a proper support order. And on obtaining the initial support order proceeded first to appeal and then to vary the order.

"This case has proceeded over 8 years with Beth Richardson receiving a mere $15,250 in support payments. Mr. Richardson has crafted a life of luxury and style while pretending that he does not have the money or the assets to pay his wife after 24 years.

"Your Honour, Beth Richardson has been in the Ontario Courts 36 times without any resolution that has benefited her.

"This motion is for an order appointing Samuel Leonard as receiver of the income and assets of Tom Richardson until all the arrears of support have been paid and security for all future payments is posted. What is different in this motion is that the request is for an order requiring third parties who benefit the support debtor to pay up an amount equivalent to the benefit derived.

"Your Honour, this motion is for an order requiring Heather Marshall, Melissa Rothbart, and Andrew Hall to submit a monthly statement of all bills, invoices, and accounts expended on behalf of Thomas Richardson and such other persons as the Receiver may determine who have likewise expended money on behalf of Thomas Richardson.

"And to the extent of each expense, Your Honour, I request an order that Heather Marshall, Melissa Rothbart and Andrew Hall, and such other persons as the Receiver may identify do pay over to the Receiver on behalf of Beth Richardson such amounts as the Receiver may determine having regard to a base amount determined under the Office of the Superintendent in Bankruptcy guidelines.

"Your Honour, I now wish to go through all the pleadings to show, by inference, that Thomas Richardson planned each step of the way to the point where the present laws of protection for spousal creditors have and continue to be defeated."

"Mr. Jordan. I have read some of your 4250 pages. Before I let you proceed, I want to hear from Mr. Schwabus first."

"Your Honour, I don't think you have to read 4250 pages to know what Mr. Jordan is asking for is unprecedented.

"He has no statute upon which he can rely.

"He has no case law; I repeat, no case law that he can hang his hat on.

"He has no authority whatsoever to suggest that this court has the jurisdiction to make the order he wants.

"Your Honour, I can save you hours and hours of your time listening to Mr. Jordan, let alone reading all this material.

"Your Honour, Mr. Jordan wants you to appoint a receiver and make orders against Heather Marshall, Melissa Rothbart, and Andrew Hall. The court does not have the facility to monitor these individuals. The court does not the financial resource to monitor the receiver. The court does not have the money to pay the receiver.

"The court is asked to make orders compelling them to supply information and payments for contributions to Mr. Richardson. Simply, Your Honour, the court cannot monitor this operation. That is exactly why Parliament and the province of Ontario have not legislated accountability against third parties who may assist the support payor. Simply, Your Honour, she has no case."

"Any introductory reply, Mr. Jordan? Where are you going, Mr. Jordan? Is not Mr. Schwabus right? There are no statutes governing this situation. There are no reported cases as he has pointed out. There are no precedents. It seems you have a steep hill to climb if I were to grant you this relief. I really don't want to read 4250 pages when as Mr. Schwabus put it, 'you don't have a case.'"

"Yes, Your Honour, I wish to reply."

"OK Mr. Jordan, Please proceed."

"Thank you, Your Honour. I have three points to make in reply.

"First, I don't need a statute or a precedent case to win this motion. Just because there is no statute or just because there are no precedent cases does not mean, respectfully, that the court has no remedy. How else is our law to develop if courts stood back and waited for Parliament to enact specific legislation? The fact that there is no specific statutory remedy protecting the spousal creditor is no bar to the availability of an equitable remedy.

"However, there is legislation. I refer you to the Courts of Justice Act wherein as you know this court has the jurisdiction to appoint a receiver where it is 'just or convenient' to do so. Courts in Ontario and elsewhere in Canada appoint receivers all the time to protect secured and unsecured creditors. Mrs. Richardson is a special unsecured creditor. Under our laws, she is a support creditor. Her claims, if Mr. Richardson were to go bankrupt, would continue. Respectfully, Your Honour, this court does have jurisdiction.

"Second, the facts, in this case, are outrageous and egregious. They cry out for relief. This case started over 8 years ago. Thirty-six court appearances later, and with this hearing, being the 37th, Mrs. Richardson is nowhere. Mr. Richardson continues to live a high lifestyle despite his purported drop in income. He has and continues to be unjustly enriched by friends and colleagues who shelter his wealth and convey benefits that one would consider luxurious.

"And last, You, Your Honour are facing the horns of a dilemma. Follow the existing law, and there is none, and dismiss the motion or make new law to rectify a wrong that has been committed by Thomas Richardson. In short, the law cannot suffer a wrong without a remedy. This court can provide that remedy.

"Now, Your Honour, I wish to proceed.

"To highlight and emphasize these outrageous facts, I need to start from the beginning.

"Your Honour, I have prepared a chronological chart starting in August 2008 when the parties decided to separate and live separate lives. It appears at Tab A of the Compendium Book 1. There are four books in the Compendium, and nine books of evidence. I ask permission to post the chronology on the court's monitor so that everyone can see each step of the way.

"Your Honour, there is a mountain of paper in front of you. I suggest you place the nine books of evidence over to the right so that you can review any particular document at will or later as required.

"The Compendium contains extracts of the more important documents needed for this application. Book 1 on the Compendium is starting point. I would refer you to Tab A again. Tab A lists all the material dates and those with an asterisk in front of the date referred to court attendances and examinations.

"For your convenience, and that of Mr. Schwabus, I have copied the chronology onto a USB and wish to display it on the court's monitor. With Your Honour's permission, I would like to ask the registrar to open the monitor for everyone in the courtroom to see."

"Yes, please do Mr. Registrar."

There it was for the whole world to see on a 75-inch screen: date, description, and result with footnotes directed to the documents in the Compendium and in the books of evidence.

For unknown reasons, it took almost two years before Mrs. Richardson saw a courtroom. Mrs. Richardson first retained Heidi Matthews in January 2008. As you can see, the first court appearance was on March 11, 2009, where Mrs. Richardson requested an interim support order of $5,000 monthly.

Macy Schwabus stands up. "Your Honour, I don't think that it is necessary for Mr. Jordan to review each date with you. The record speaks for itself. You have all the court filings and rulings in the Compendium. I accept the chronology prepared by Mr. Jordan."

"Well, Mr. Jordan."

"Your Honour, this case is fact driven. The facts are outrageous. You cannot get the flavor of the hostility, outrage, and frustration without knowing what happened at each step of the proceedings. We have booked the whole day in court for this hearing, Your Honour. I wish to use the day for my presentation."

"Carry on Mr. Jordan."

At the end of the morning, Eli sums up his presentation:
- This case is in its 8th year running without resolution.
- After 9 attempts in securing an interim order, Mr. Justice Fairworthy ordered Mr. Richardson to pay $5,000 monthly in 2010. His Honour

followed the Spousal Support Advisory Guidelines to arrive at a fair amount.

- Mr. Richardson appealed that ruling. In December 2012, he conceded and abandoned his appeal.
- Once the parties separated in 2009, Mr. Richardson closed out all joint bank accounts and terminated all joint credit cards.
- Mrs. Richardson had no bank account, had no credit card in her name alone, and had no means of supporting herself following the separation.
- Mrs. Richardson was a homemaker and raised two children.
- Mrs. Richardson was middle-aged, did not have a university education, and had a difficult time entering the workforce.
- Since 2012, Mr. Richardson owes over $250,000 plus costs exceeding $110,000.
- Mr. Richardson has paid $15,250 on account.
- Mr. Richardson's net income dropped from $250,000 in 2007 to $30,000 to $45,000 from 2008 to the present.
- Mr. Richardson has been on 5 examinations in aid of execution, 4 of which were no-shows or adjourned because he was late or did not have the documents necessary for the examination.
- Mr. Richardson has been held in contempt of court 3 times and has served 6 months for one of his contempt orders;
- Mr. Richardson lives in a 3-bedroom penthouse in Mid-town Toronto. He has no lease and pays no rent. The condominium appears to be owned by his long-time friend Andy Hall.
- Mr. Richardson lost in driver's licence as a result of an enforcement from the Family Responsibility Office; however, that does not deter him from driving his BMW.
- Mr. Richardson drives a 2015 BMW 750. The BMW is leased to his live-in friend Melissa Rothbart.
- Mr. Richardson lost his passport as a result of an enforcement by the Family Responsibility Office.
- Yet, Mr. Richardson travels to central Europe once a year for 3 months on some other passport.
- Mr. Richardson has displayed 'bad faith'. He knew his wife needed support from the moment he left the family home. Mrs. Richardson is

entitled to a full recovery of her costs, and if he does not pay them, one way or another, the court should sentence him again.

- Simply put Your Honour, Mr. Richardson has stonewalled Mrs. Richardson in disclosing assets and property in the expectation that she will submit to the judicial system and walk away.

"I got the picture, Mr. Jordan. Thank you."

"Mr. Schwabus, let's take a break over lunch. Let's reconvene at 2:30 PM."

The court registrar announces the lunch break. All rise.

2:30 PM

The court re-assembles.

Mr. Schwabus stands and addresses the court.

"May it please, Your Honour, Mr. Jordan has made out a case where there is no precedent. My client has complied with all orders to the best of his ability. He has purged his contempt; he had paid what he could from his income."

"Mr. Schwabus, how do you explain Mr. Richardson's lifestyle? It seems that Mr. Richardson has all the benefits of a middle-class lifestyle without the burden of payment. Can you explain that to me?"

"Your Honour, I want to review with you Mr. Richardson's tax returns over the last 5 years. You will see that the bottom line is that there is no surplus money with which to pay Mrs. Richardson."

"I know that, Mr. Schwabus. But you haven't answered my question. Shall I repeat it?"

"Yes, Your Honour."

"Mr. Schwabus, how do you explain Mr. Richardson's lifestyle?"

"He has friends that are prepared to support him. These are gifts. But Your Honour, I would like to challenge this new type of receivership order that Mr. Jordan proposes. The court does not have the power to order third parties to obey an order that is going to be impossible to enforce."

"Mr. Schwabus, are you telling me that a person who earns about $36,000 to $40,000 a year can afford to drive a BMW sports car, have Blue Jay tickets behind the catcher, live in a penthouse of 3500 square feet, and travel to England and France every year while his ex relies on her aging parents for support? Am I missing something?"

"Shouldn't these third parties who benefit Mr. Richardson pay an amount over a certain threshold? Cannot Mr. Jordan use the Superintendent's Guidelines to restrict a base amount for living standards and then everything over that amount becomes payable by the person or company that extends the benefit to him?"

Pause.

"I would like to take an early break to speak to my client."

"That's sounds like a good idea, Mr. Schwabus. When would you like to reconvene?"

"Tomorrow morning?"

"No, let's reconvene in one hour. I'm here for the day, and I am not available for this matter tomorrow. You and Mr. Jordan can work out something. I will be in chambers if you need me."

"OK."

"All rise."

The End